Crazy Buffet Club

A Collection of Stories

Copyright 2018 by JimmyLee Smith

Introduction copyright 2018 by Calvin Beam

ALL RIGHTS RESERVED

No portion of this book may be reproduced in any form without permission from the publisher, except as permitted by U.S. copyright law. For permissions contact: info@crazybuffet.club

"Martyred Justice Introduction" by Blaire Adams. Copyright 2018 by Blaire Adams. Printed by permission of Blaire Adams.

"In for a Penny" by Calvin Beam. Copyright 2018 by Calvin Beam. Printed by permission of Calvin Beam.

"The Quantum Mechanic" by Calvin Beam. Copyright 2018 by Calvin Beam. Printed by permission of Calvin Beam.

"Fireflies" by Elijah David. Copyright 2018 by Elijah David. Printed by permission of Elijah David.

"A Swarm of Flies" by Max Hernandez. Copyright 2018 by Max Hernandez. Printed by permission of Max Hernandez.

"It Came" by Jonathon Hixson. Copyright 2018 by Jonathon Hixson. Printed by permission of Jonathon Hixson.

"Letters from the Front" by Jonathon Hixson. Copyright 2018 by Jonathon Hixson. Printed by permission of Jonathon Hixson.

"Cryptic Case of Christof Kiran" by J. Smith Kirkland. Copyright 2018 by J. Smith Kirkland. Printed by permission of J. Smith Kirkland.

"Gretz" by J. Smith Kirkland. Copyright 2018 by J. Smith Kirkland. Printed by permission of J. Smith Kirkland.

"Busted at Bingo" by Kelle Z. Riley. Copyright 2018 by Kelle Z. Riley. Printed by permission of Kelle Z. Riley.

"The End Game" by Peter Sculley. Copyright 2018 by Peter Sculley. Printed by permission of Peter Sculley.

"Burnished Obsidian" by Gary Sedlacek. Copyright 2018 by Gary Sedlacek. Printed by permission of Gary Sedlacek.

Cover Art by Meredith Hodges-Boos

www.crazybuffet.club
www.instagram.com/crazyBuffetClub

Dedication

For Joe Petree (1934-2017), who steered our group skillfully, gave generously, accepted graciously, and persevered courageously.

Introduction

Once there was a group of writers. They wrote in different genres. They wrote in different styles. They were very different in age, experience, political outlook, and their stance on the Oxford comma. (Note to editor: Do not change the punctuation in that sentence.) But they were all writers. And they were all perhaps a little crazy each in their own way.

A couple of times a month, they gathered at a buffet restaurant to eat and to talk about writing and life in general. Their time together inspired them in their craft. To this day they deny that their group had any connection with the fact that at least two of the buffets where they gathered went out of business.

They criticized one another, brainstormed together, laughed as much as they disagreed and shared what they learned in a group that's been going strong for more than a decade. They've greeted new members enthusiastically and said goodbye reluctantly to those who've become our friends.

Then one day, one of them said, "Let's make some short stories, and put them together in a collection." They all agreed this would be a good idea. And they did. This is it.

As a member of this crazy buffet club, I hope you enjoy our collection of stories. If you find an author whose style you like, who stirs your emotion with a phrase, who plants a story in your mind that you remember long after you've put the book aside, we'll call that a success.

And just one more thing to note, the group of writers is based in Hixson, TN. They decided that the profits from their collection of stories would go to support a regional arts or writing program. The profits from sales of the first edition will go to the Young Southern Student Writers sponsored by the Southern Lit Alliance and UTC's Department of English to help offset the cost of the awards ceremony they hold each year.

Table of Contents

Busted at Bingo 1
   by Kelle Z. Riley
Cryptic Case of Christof Kiran 13
   by J. Smith Kirkland
The End Game 27
   by Peter Sculley
Fireflies 52
   by Elijah David
Gretz 65
   by J. Smith Kirkland
In for a Penny 71
   by Calvin Beam
It Came 75
   by Jonathan Hixson
Letter from the Front Lines 77
   by Jonathan Hixson
The Quantum Mechanic 78
   by Calvin Beam
A Swarm Of Flies 98
   by Max Hernandez
Burnished Obsidian 110
   by Gary Sedlacek
Martyred Justice 131
   by Blaire Adams
About The Authors 136

Busted at Bingo

by Kelle Z. Riley

A little over fifteen years ago…

"You talk funny."

Bree stared at her gap-toothed, six-year-old cousin and resisted the urge to tell him he was the one with the funny accent.

"Travis, don't poke fun at your cousin," his mother said from the front passenger seat of the car. "It's not nice."

"But it's true," Travis insisted.

"It's okay, Aunt Sherry." Bree felt a surge of pride in the patience she'd gained since becoming a teenager earlier this year. She smiled at Travis and twisted toward him as far as the seatbelt would allow. "Trav, I sound funny because I grew up in another state. Want to guess which one?"

Travis blinked at her and narrowed his eyes as if considering. Bree took that for a yes.

"Here's a hint. I come from a state that is round on the ends and high in the middle. Now guess."

His brow puckered. "Huh? You mean high like mountains and stuff? But how can a state be round?"

Bree simply smiled and pulled a notepad out of the backpack at her feet. "Like this," she drew two circles with a wide space between them and passed the note to Travis. "Round on the ends and high," she wrote the word "hi" between the circles, "in the middle."

"O-Hi-O. I get it. Ohio." Travis bounced in his seat. "You sound funny because you're from Ohio. That makes her a Yankee, right, mom?"

"It does," answered Bree's Aunt Sherry. "But we love her anyway."

"Tell me another one, cousin Bree."

"All right." Bree pretended to think hard while she watched Travis wiggle in anticipation. "You, your mom, and grandma are all from Chattanooga, right? So what did Tennessee?"

"What did Tennessee?" he repeated, puzzled.

"The same as Arkansas," replied Bree. "Get it? See? Saw?"

Travis burst into giggles, his concern over his Yankee cousin's accent forgotten. "Why is six afraid of seven?" he asked when he caught his breath. "Because…"

"…seven ate nine," Bree and Travis finished in unison.

Gravel crunched under the tires as Bree's grandmother pulled into the lot next to the community center, signaling the end of the joke fest. Bree grabbed her backpack and exited the car, falling into step with her grandmother while Travis and his mom followed.

"You don't have to play bingo with us old folks,"

Gram said, smiling down at her. "You can find a seat anywhere."

Bree shrugged. "I don't mind." As an only child, she'd spent more than her share of time with adults, so a round or two of bingo didn't daunt her. "I'll stay with you for a while if that's okay."

Inside, the community center hummed with the voices of dozens of people—mostly senior citizens—crammed around rows of long, narrow tables. A deserted snack bar occupied one corner. The front was dominated by a raised platform with a giant cage of bingo balls and a lightboard for showing the numbers once they were drawn.

"You may change your tune about playing." Gram's eyes narrowed as she led Bree to one of the few open seats left. Aunt Sherry snagged a seat on the other side of Gram, leaving Bree to sit next to a curly-haired stranger with thick glasses.

Gram gestured to the woman, whose bulk overflowed the folding chair just like her bingo cards overflowed the space in front of her.

"Bree, this is Bertha Hollingsworth. Bertha, my granddaughter Bree Mayfield-Watson."

"Hello, Mrs. Hollingsworth."

"Mrs. Hollingsworth was my mother-in-law, Lord bless her soul." The woman chuckled, multiple chins waggling with mirth. "You can call me Bertie—Big Bertie—like everyone else." Big Bertie patted the seat next to her and Bree obligingly sat.

"You are such a cute little mite. Stick with us, darlin'

and we'll smooth out that Yankee drawl of yours and make you a perfect southern lady." Bree suppressed a shudder as Bertie Hollingsworth pinched her cheeks. Had the woman even looked at her? Bree wasn't cute. She wasn't little. And, as much as she loved her Grandma, she wasn't interested in changing her accent just to fit in. She bit her tongue—figuratively, of course—and kept respectfully silent.

Big Bertie plucked a slightly grubby stuffed duck from its place of honor in the middle of the bingo cards and waggled it in front of Bree's face. "This is my lucky-ducky, Quackers. She always comes with me to bingo. You can look, but don't touch."

"No ma'am," Bree said, casting a glance down the length of the table. Bertie wasn't the only one with a lucky charm. Dolls, toys, decorated pens to "dab" at the bingo squares and every other kind of talisman sat in front of the players.

On her other side, Gram arranged her cards and markers in a no-nonsense line that left no room for chance. "Bree, do you want to have some cards of your own, or will you help me?"

Bree pulled two of Gram's cards toward her and accepted a marker.

"My granddaughter Bree gets straight A's in her science classes." As Gram addressed the table in general, she dropped an affectionate arm over Bree's shoulder and gave her a wink. "Like her, I'm not a big believer in luck. But Big Bertie does seem to have the devil's own. Maybe Mr. Quackers will spread some of his good luck to the rest of us."

"I wouldn't count on it," muttered Aunt Sherry so softly Bree almost didn't hear her.

Bertie sniffed and dabbed beneath her glasses at her eyes. "Mabel-May Mayfield, I never took you for a sore loser. Especially not in front of this impressionable young girl."

Gram sighed. "It's a joke, Bertie. Although maybe I *should* get a good luck charm of my own." Gram leaned toward the grubby duck, but Bertie pulled it out of reach.

"Hands off Quackers." She rummaged in a bag at her feet and extracted a large stuffed mouse. "I'll let you borrow Squeaky." She passed the toy to Gram, who placed it between herself and Bree.

"I guess it can't hurt." Gram shrugged, but looked unconvinced.

"At least you fit in with the rest of the table," Bree whispered. She nodded toward the toys in front of other players. "Is it always like this?"

"Bingo? You bet. It's crazy at times. But there's snacks, more gossip than a girl your age should have to hear, and a chance to win a little money. Not a bad way to pass the afternoon." She lowered her voice. "If you get tired of listening to Big Bertie bend your ear about her family, I'll understand. That woman can talk the ears off a Billy goat. Take yourself off in a corner and listen to your music anytime you want to, honey."

A microphone crackled to life and everyone's attention turned to the makeshift stage. A dapper elderly man with a cloud of frizzy white hair positioned himself behind the cage of bingo balls. Bright red suspenders stood out like narrow stripes against his white shirt. He gave the cage a twirl. "Is everyone ready?"

Amid the chorus of welcoming cries, Big Bertha held Quackers up to her lips and kissed the grubby duck. "Bring me luck," she whispered to him.

On stage the caller ran a hand through his hair then patted it into place. "Let's get started," he announced and pulled a ball from the bingo cage. "I-twenty-two."

* * * *

Two games later, the caller's rapid-fire litany of numbers had Bree wondering how the ladies with a dozen or more cards managed. She kept up with her two cards—neither of them winning any of the games—but was losing interest in the whole process.

Worse, Big Bertha seemed to think Bree wanted to hear her whole family history. Nieces, nephews, aunts, cousins, children of all ages seemed to spring from the Hollingsworth family tree like... well like the little, bitty branches of Gram's peach tree that smacked her in the face when Bree walked by it, her nose buried in a book.

"Bree," asked Big Bertie, "you must be what, thirteen?"

"Yes ma'am," she replied politely, grabbing the dabber and marking the square for G-52 as the caller announced it. "My birthday was in—"

"B-13, ladies and gentlemen. B-13," announced the caller.

"Bingo!" Big Bertie popped up from her chair and waved an attendant over to check her card.

"Like I said," Gram whispered in Bree's ear "she has the devil's luck."

Bree held her own for a few more rounds, during which Big Bertha won more than she lost and Gram and Aunt Sherry both studied their cards with grim determination. Finally, Bree excused herself and went in search of snacks.

Ten minutes later, she settled into a quiet corner, her back to the wall and pulled a book from her backpack. She sipped her Coke and munched on chips while delving into the text on radio waves her dad had given her. Soon, she shoved the chips aside in favor of a small radio. As she listened through her headphones, she popped the front panel of the radio off and studied the circuit board inside, alternating between looking at the board and referring to her book. She used a tiny screwdriver to make adjustments, noting the changes in her notebook.

"Whatcha doin'?" Travis grabbed her half eaten bag of chips and plopped down beside her.

"I'm learning how this radio works. Want to help me?"

He scrunched his nose. "Don't you just turn in on and pick a station?"

Over the hum of conversation from the bingo players, Bree launched into a discussion of frequencies, amplitudes and wave functions. When Travis's eyes glazed over, she gave up. "It's nothing, Squirt. Just some stuff my dad and I do together."

"Like fishing and working on trucks?" Travis asked.

Bree nodded, resisting the temptation to show off her knowledge of car engines and drive systems. Travis wasn't likely to be any more impressed by the physics of propulsion then he was by the science of radio waves. When it came to her scientific interests, Bree didn't fit in with kids her own age. Much less younger ones like Travis.

That was part of the reason mom had sent her to Gram's for the summer. She'd hoped Bree would become less of a geek, not a bigger one. Thank goodness dad had slipped the textbook and radio into her backpack when mom wasn't looking or Bree might have gone crazy over the six week trip.

When Travis ambled away—taking the remainder of Bree's chips with him—she returned her focus to the radio. A few quarter turns of dials later, static crackled through the earphones. Another adjustment and the static resolved into words.

"Iris, my eighteen year old granddaughter, is going to Chattanooga State in the fall," said a voice Bree recognized as Big Bertie's. Even in this far corner of the room she couldn't get away from the chatty senior citizen.

"I-eighteen," announced the caller, his voice sounding muffled because of her headphones. "I-eighteen."

Bree looked up to see him spinning the cage again.

"O-sixty-three."

"Bingo!" Bertie jumped to her feet with a surprising agility given her bulk. She waved her card and Bree winced at the sound of the woman's voice coming clear through the headphones and muffled through...

Wait. The sounds *from the room* were muffled. But Big Bertie's voice was clear. As if broadcast over the radio.

Bree listened for a while longer. Yes. Bertie's voice, chattering about children, grandchildren and extended family members sounded through the radio via the earphones. Bree abandoned the textbook and scribbled in her notebook, transcribing Big Bertie's chatter as best as she could.

The bingo caller announced another number and Bertie popped up again. Bree frowned, her mind spinning. What had he just called? N-forty-two. She wrote it down.

Scanning Big Bertie's transcribed chatter, Bree began fitting pieces of a puzzle together. *Nancy, that's my forty-two year old, was telling me just the other day…*

Bree gripped her pencil tighter. Bertha Hollingsworth wasn't lucky. She was cheating.

* * * *

Several games later, Bree was convinced she'd stumbled on a cheating ring consisting of—at least—the caller and Big Bertha Hollingsworth. After listening for more clues from Bertie—names that started with B, I, N, G or O followed by numbers—and matching those verbal clues to the squares announced by the caller, Bree had enough evidence.

Plus, after scouring the textbook her dad had sent, Bree had been able to confirm that her adjustments to her radio would allow it to pick up signals from a hand-held device.

She shoved the book and notes into her backpack, stuck the radio carefully into her pocket and walked over to where Gram, Aunt Sherry and Big Bertie sat. She slid between Gram and Bertie. "Are you having fun," she asked, directing her voice toward Quackers the stuffed duck.

Her own voice reverberated through her tiny headset.

Gram answered with a tight lipped *umm-hmm*. Faintly, through the speakers, Bree picked up Gram's voice. She removed her earpiece and tugged on Gram's sleeve. "Can I talk to you for a minute?"

Gram gathered her cards. "Sure, honey. I need to get some new cards anyway." Together Gram and Bree walked toward the table selling the bingo cards. On the way, Bree told Gram of her suspicions in whispered tones.

They bypassed the cashier and Gram pulled Bree into the parking lot. Humid summer heat slammed into them as they exited the cool darkness of the community center. "Do you mean to tell me that Bertha Hollingsworth is cheating at bingo?" Gram demanded once the door to the center closed behind them.

Bree chewed her lip against the anger in Gram's voice, but nodded. She showed Gram her notes, sure of her research. "You can listen for yourself, if you want to," she said pulling the radio out of her pocket. "My radio is picking up signals—probably from a walkie-talkie handset hidden inside Quackers. Mrs. Hollingsworth will say a name starting with B, I, N, G, or O followed by a number. Then the caller will call that combination of letter and number. Sometimes he does it immediately. Sometimes he waits for one round. Then either that round or the next, Mrs. Hollingsworth will hit a bingo."

Gram took the radio, listened for several long minutes, then handed the radio and notebook back to Bree. "Young lady, it's time you and I found the security guard. We've just cracked the mystery of Big Bertie's lucky streak." She wrapped an arm around Bree's shoulders. "That's my girl," Gram said with a smile.

* * * *

Two days later, Bree sat on Gram's couch, sharing a bowl of popcorn with her cousin Travis. Aunt Sherry flipped the TV to a local news station. On screen, the anchor launched into a story detailing the arrest of several thieves accused of robbing bingo games throughout the Chattanooga area. Citing an unnamed source for uncovering the ring, the news anchor went on to say the thieves were part of a larger group who'd stolen thousands of dollars from communities across several states.

"My goodness," Aunt Sherry said, when mug shots of Big Bertie and the dapper caller in red suspenders flashed across the screen. "Who would have imagined such a thing. In our bingo hall, no less. I wonder how they caught them?"

Gram shook her head. "It took somebody pretty smart and special to uncover their crimes," Gram said, sneaking a sly wink at Bree when Aunt Sherry's back was turned. "Too bad we'll probably never know who."

Bree flashed Gram a secret smile and returned to her popcorn.

Cryptic Case of Christof Kiran

by J. Smith Kirkland

In The Beginning

My life began the day I first put paint to canvas, and when I met him. I knew his portrait would be my greatest masterpiece.

He asked me once, "why do you paint?"

I could have rambled on about my philosophies, talked of how in the age of binary, the old ways of art have never been lost. Oil, acrylics, clay, metal, glass. They will remain timeless. Each new digital advancement created a great new tool to use for art. No artist would turn down a new medium to try, or to combine with an old one.

I imagine Vincent himself would have delighted in photoshop, but the old mediums are never lost. I love my digital camera. It's a big bulky one with large interchangeable lenses. I use it for specific styles. I also love the camera on my wrist phone. Both have a purpose and create their own art. Both excellent mediums. I love photography, but paint is my main love. The smell of the paint, the texture, pushing it across a canvas or piece of wood. It's sensual and spiritual. The camera they say can capture the soul, but paint captures something more, the essence of a person. That's what I wanted to capture on canvas, his essence, his humanity.

But I knew he was looking for a more technical answer to the question. We had those types of discussions from time to time.

"I understand how mixing the different colors creates the hue you desire, but why do you select that hue? It's not exactly the same as the subject, but you seem to mix the paint so carefully to get a precise color."

"I paint what I see."

"But that's not what it looks like."

"You have to look at the beauty beyond the colors"

These sort of answers never satisfied him. His world was science and reasoning. He needed to dissect art down into components that could be understood logically, reconfigured into new implementations, new forms. Just like most of society, he was taught that knowing how things work is knowledge. Though most were content to just enjoy the products of technological knowledge, like wrist phones and other digital toys. They don't really need the knowledge, just the technology. For so many, it's as if history began with the first generation of *cryptocritters*.

History of the World

Cryptocritters started out as a game. A digital pasttime for people that once would have collected *beanie babies*. Who would have thought the game would evolve into what it did? *Cryptocritters* were not simply a computer program that you had to digitally 'feed' and 'pet', and then could just reinstall forgetting to do that for too long.

These new *cryptocritters* were based on the technology for cryptocurrencies. Each one unique. Each protected by digital security that tracks ownership so it can't be replicated, stolen, or destroyed. But they were more than just another cryptocoin too; they also used the latest DNA algorithms. That means owners can 'breed' two *cryptocritters*. The result being a new genetically unique offspring.

At first, owners could connect their pet with other *cryptocritters* to make friends for them. The cryptocritters could play games together, send each other messages, like each other's photos. They ruled social media. Additional features were added constantly. The DNA algorithms could initially pass attributes along to the offspring like hair color, hair texture, eye shape, eye color, and other graphical features. Eventually, personality traits were added, and talents like being better at one game than another. For example, one *cryptocritter* may have a natural talent for jumping high, but another may have to practice jumping for some time before it gets good at it.

And the games evolved also. Educational games about science and math led to *cryptocritter* talents in those areas. While some were born with more initial talent, all *cryptocritter* were only limited by how fast they learned, not how much they could learn. *Cryptocritter* camps were even invented. Owners could connect their *cryptocritter* online to sites that trained them for games, help them jump higher, or answer more science and math questions correctly. *Cryptocritter* owners were the new soccer moms, pushing their "child" to go to the best *crittercamps*, play on the best *critterteams*, go to the best *critterschools*, have play dates and breed with other *cryptocritters* that also came from good breeding.

The *cryptocritter* phenomenon moved like a wildfire across the globe. They were traded like gold. Breeds were created. Lineages were tracked. Purebreds were auctioned off for tens of thousands. Then the next evolution happened. The *cryptocritters* were no longer confined to the tiny screen on the owner's phone. With 3D printing and chip technology, they were uploaded into physical avatars. At first they were miniature desktop hard plastic robot toys. But owners wanted more. If the digital DNA algorithms had evolved to the 3D printer, and the 3D printer had evolved to print synthetic skin, noses, and ears for burn patients, then why not more realistic feeling cryptopets to hold in your hand. Soft synthetic skin and hair soon covered the most desirable and expensive *cryptocritters*.

The next level came quickly again. With the loss of a beloved family pet, a real live animal, their owners would have a replica *cryptocritters* created. Full sized pets were created. But to make the new replacement as most like their deceased loved one as possible, they needed more than the digital the DNA algorithm. Actual DNA from the animal was processed and decoded in order to create additional digital DNA information for the new *cryptocritters*. This continued to make each *cryptocritters* extremely unique, and the ones created from purebred live animals, were bred together to keep the lineage. Under protest, The American Kennel Club eventually started new branches to track the *cryptocritter* breeds.

These new cryptodoppelgangers were physical companions for their owners, but their profile still existed in the digital world, and could be uplinked to socialize and play the *cryptocritters* games online. And they continued to learn. Owners had debates on which were better at math games, cryptocats or cryptodogs. Which breed was better at teaching your kid math and how to program computers, a Black Labrador or Golder Retriever. The *cryptocritters* were getting smarter and smarter.

After several unexplained sales of some very valuable *cryptocritters*, the owners accused the *cryptocritters* company of employees hacking into the user accounts and stealing their precious family members, or the security software being vulnerable to terrorist. The company denied any wrongdoing, and quickly issued press releases that said there was a bug in the most recent release of the user account software, and that it had been quickly fixed, and the programmer had resigned.

But this explanation did not appease the imagination

of the robot revolution conspiracy theorist. They had already refused to allow their refrigerator to go online and order refills to be delivered by drones. They would not ride in self driving cars that could give you suggestions on restaurants you would like, or which music you like, or which showstores were displaying products you might like to check out and have delivered. Now the theorists' worse prediction seemed to be inevitable. There were theories that the *cryptocritters* themselves had started manipulating their own value, forming corporations, taking percentages of each *cryptocritters* sale, and creating new avatars for themselves that were indistinguishable from humans. Most people thought their existence was just crazy conspiracy theory, but the truth was cryptohumans were everywhere.

That's where my story begins.

History of Christof Kiran

He was different, everyone just said he was brilliant, and they overlooked his quirks. He had built an amazing business in just a few years. He was a leader in the expanding society of philanthropreneurs. He and his kind use their resources to create social change that is scalable and sustainable. Their contribution goes beyond providing temporary fixes. Instead of spending resources for the purchase of medicine and food, philanthropreneurs seek to eradicate the problems of hunger and sickness.

I suppose that as an artist, I more or less chose being poor over following rules and expectations, but these people were different. Their passion was to make the world a better place for all of us, and they didn't have to be poor to achieve it. He could have been wealthy, but chose to keep just what he needed. He lived comfortably, but not immoderately. His enterprise and generosity both unassailable. His confidence presented as kindness, not arrogance. He was indeed brilliant. But there was more. I could see it.

"I want to paint you," I think were the first words I said to him.

He just smiled, "I have mirrors, I don't need a portrait of myself."

"I wouldn't be for you."

I think that confused his genius enough that he stayed around for more conversation. He eventually agreed to sit for some sketches; we both agreed it could not be done from photos. And he said if those sketches convinced him, he would sit for the painting.

He was not a striking action movie hero, or even the perfect looking guy from the romantic comedy. But the symmetry people associate with beauty was almost there. His skin was flawless, except for one tiny patch of eczema just below his right jawline. I painted it in, covered it, repainted it. I was never happy with it, even when I had it looking exactly like the real patch.

"I will make it a tattoo", I thought, "but what would he get as a tattoo?"

It was a decision I put off until the rest of the portrait was complete. We talked while I sketched and painted. I thought maybe as I learned more about him, and not just his public persona that I would conclude the perfect tattoo.

"Why do you paint?"

"I was made to paint; it's in my DNA, along with a sweet tooth and synthesia that makes makes me sneeze when I step from a low lit room into the sunlight."

"That's a unique trait."

"There are a few of us. I suppose business savvy and the quest for knowledge must be in your DNA. Your father was a scientist? Doctor?"

"I'm told he was a social rights leader."

"You're told?"

"I don't really remember him. I have picture of when he was young, but I was raised by my mother."

"My mother made the best sugar cookies. I can still see her mixing up the batter in a big yellow bowl, and the color and smell of *McCormick's Vanilla* flavoring. Did your mom bake?"

His countenance changed. He answered only with a short, "No."

He never really mentioned either one of them again. I had lots of theories, but decided to postpone any further questions. I didn't try to pry any of those answers from his locked emotions; I didn't want to risk not finishing my masterpiece.

I decided on a *cryptocritter* tattoo. Retro. But what kind. Cat? He is sorta like a cat. Aloof, smart, agile. But just can't see him getting a cutesy cat tattoo. I eventually chose the *cryptocritter* I had purchased myself. It's one of those old retro small hard plastic ones. A dragon.

I didn't know what he would think of me adding the tattoo. I hoped he didn't find it insulting, or think that I thought the eczema made him less beautiful. I didn't. And besides, the patch was almost dragon shaped. I really thought the painted dragon had revealed more than his soul, his essence. I was pleased, and it turned out he liked it too. He surprised me one day when he walked in with an actual tattoo imitating the one in the portrait.

The Evolution of the World

His business was involved with providing medical supplies for hospitals that provided free care for the poorest of society. That's how he first found the crypto revolution theorist. Most of the world organizations had cut back little by little on the information about population. There were no longer government censuses.

The old data was still online, but not a lot of new data. Crypto-revolution theorist would count newborns in hospital nursery. They would figure out what time of day all newborns would be there. If caught looking too long, people would ask which is yours. There was a list of answers that usually stopped more questions. "I'm not sure it's mine," or "the one not crying."

He told me one day that he was beginning to believe it was more than a conspiracy theory. He had started going to the major hospitals himself, and asking if he could get stats on birth and death records. The main reaction from the staff was, "Why would you want that?" To which he said the reply, "I am fascinated by numbers and patterns" always seemed to be a good enough answer. Once they figure out who he was, they would scan his face for recognition, print him out a badge, and send him, unescorted to the archives.

I watched in fascination as his astute intellect took on a mystery. I never felt that drive to acquire knowledge. I tended to look for the beauty. The thousands of colors in a raindrop, the way wheat moves in the wind like it's rocking you to sleep, the way a snowflake melts on a finger tip. I was seeing a new divergent beauty through the kindness emoted from his intents. How do you paint enlightenment?

He started interacting more and more with the crypto-revolution theorists. He said they asked him a lot of question. He thinks it was to make sure he was human.

"Oh yeah, there are 'tells' that have been used by your conspiracy friends for a long time. One of them is the smell of vanilla. Did they ask you that one?"

"No."

"They probably forgot to; so excited by who you are."

He didn't like notoriety or me reminding him of it, but he knew he was famous, and he knew why. It pleased him most that he was known for his compassion, and not wealth. But much later he told me that they did bring up vanilla, and he had just echoed what I had said about my mother making cookies.

The Evolution of Christoff Kiran

One day after he met with the theorist about some new leaked messages between the *cryptocritter* company and a government agency, he seemed less excited about his investigations, and more sad. He told me all about how there was no longer doubt that there were cryptopeople, made basically from the same DNA as humans, but their brains were controlled with computer chips. Their DNA, a hash of digital and human. Basically a new life form. I think he was surprised when I believed him, and calmly told him that I had heard a lot of the theories myself. They seemed logical.

"I heard they were using DNA of famous historical people. There may be another Van Gogh walking around for me to compete with."

I tried to get him to smile, turning my canvas toward him to reveal that I was painting sunflowers. No use.

"What I always wondered," I went on, "is why would they continue to use organic tissue for creating avatars. It is so fragile. Of course, with the new medical advances, you can easily replace anything that goes wrong with the organic material too, or just have your DNA repaired and let your body do the rest on its own."

He listened to me like he had never heard my voice before.

I mean, is it just to blend in with humans? I wonder if, when there are just a few humans left, if the designers will go with stronger material, like they did when they made the first little *crytocritters?*"

He didn't say anything.

"Of course," I continued, "I guess, the new stronger materials may be a lot like digital photography, and the organic material is like painting in oil. Why not have both. I mean look at you, your skin is flawless."

He walked over to his portrait hanging on my wall. He stared at it like it was a proclamation. He touched the dragon tattoo on the painting, and then on his neck.

"I'm not human?"

"Do you remember growing up, and the cookies you said your mom made? Do you remember their smell?

"No."

"They can give you a past, a history, complete with memories. The technologies are very advanced, but for some reason there are still things that are difficult to create. They are still working on perfecting olfactory memories. Soon there will be no questions to give away who is who. There are a few prototypes."

I had heard there were cryptohumans that thought they were human. I had long suspected he had no idea he wasn't. I was glad he was discovering the truth. I was happy for him, and frightened for him at the same time. I hoped it would not alter his compassion, his distinctive form of humanity. But when he looked at me with full understanding in his eyes, and a thousand colors in the tear that ran down his cheek to the tattoo just below his jawline, I knew he would be okay.

"I am not human," he said.

"No. But neither am I."

History began with *cryptocritters*. My life began the day i first put paint to canvas, and when I met him.

The End Game

by Peter Sculley

Chapter 1

They led him past a group of people to a padded chair. His face was frozen in a gentle smile. There was no fuss as he sat down, settled in, and rolled up his sleeve.

A somber mood permeated the place. A place where no one walked away untouched. The rare conversations were hushed and sporadic. An occasional cough slipped out.

Bright lights encircled his chair, high above his head. Additional chairs sat in shadows, hiding the faces of others, watching.

A lady dressed in 'scrubs' swabbed his arm with a wad of wet cotton leaving an orange hue on his skin. She reached over to the stainless steel cart and removed a small cylinder of plastic.

A gentle twist of her wrist separated the cylinder and a sliver of steel appeared. She bent over his arm and ran her fingers over the inside of his forearm.

He caught a hint of peach; shampoo? One of the few times in his life he paid scant attention to such a lovely lady.

A sharp prick took his mind off the peach scent. She slid the needle into his vein with a practiced precision; a professional.

He watched as she wrapped a wide piece of clear tape over the needle, leaving the top accessible. Connection secured.

A long tube connected to a bag of saline solution hung from a steel pole.

She removed the clamp from the end of the tube and allowed one drop of fluid to clear the path. Returning the clamp, she connected the tube to the steel in his arm. Not another drop was lost.

He felt the sweat pooling under his arms.

She removed the clamp and he could feel the coolness of the saline coursing in his arm.

Another gentle hint of peach filled his consciousness as she straightened up, a compassionate look on her face.

He looked around the room. Several people stared at him. Most pointedly ignored him. Ignoring them, he concentrated on the lady in scrubs. She hooked three bags of fluid next to the saline.

No fancy writing on these bags. Only a paper label with his name printed by hand.

A whiff of peach assailed him as she connected the new tubes to the growing jungle on his arm.

She removed the clamp on the first new bag.

A slight burning sensation told him the poison was

entering his system.

Chemo sucked!

Chapter 2

They changed the routine on his third visit.

The lady that reminded him of peaches talked to him on the way back to the treatment room. She stopped outside the door and in a soft voice said, "I know you're rather reticent about the treatments. I know you prefer to be by yourself."

He saw the 'but' coming.

"But a friend of mine is taking her first treatment and she's a bit nervous. Would you sit next to her? She probably won't talk much, but she would appreciate your presence. Just having someone there, and you're the same age group."

A dozen stations surrounded the room, each with a reclining lounge chair and room for a cart. The patients sat as far apart as possible giving the impression of privacy.

He wanted to be left alone, but he felt the pressure of helping a lady in trouble. So he told the polite lie, "Sure, be glad to."

They walked into the treatment room and a lady sat reading a magazine. She waved at the nurse, a furtive wave that the other patients missed.

He didn't miss the wave. He nodded at the lady and sat down in the recliner next to her so she sat to his left side. Another nurse wheeled in the cart with his bags of saline; and poison. One wheel of the cart gave an annoying squeal.

A few minutes later he felt the tingling of all the drugs running into his arm.

The cocktail of saline, poisons, nausea drugs, and the steroids to build him up, all fought for his attention. The nausea kicked in and kicked out. He started sweating again; side effect from the meds, not the warmth of the room.

He read his book, but couldn't tell you what he read.

A quiet voice from his left said, "Does the nausea get bad?" She spoke with a soft feminine voice, low pitched and oh so pleasant.

He lifted his head up from his book and thought of how best to answer. "Not usually. Everyone in here gets a different treatment. But the nurses have the nausea part down pretty good. You'll feel like you're floating in an ocean of drugs after awhile. And it's kind of hard on your kidneys. That's why there are so many restrooms around the treatment room. Sometimes a bout of nausea hits a few days after the treatments. You'll feel it coming on."

He glanced at her not wanting to break the protocol of privacy and thought, *Pretty lady!* She seemed content with the answer.

Some patients wanted to talk to keep their minds off what was happening to their cancer-ravaged bodies. Some brought visitors. Most wanted quiet and the privacy that no one received.

The visitors, usually spouses or progeny, talked and

talked and talked. A never ending drone against the background noise of the air conditioning system.

Almost as if the visitors felt guilty about not being sick; not sharing the treatments. They talked louder to make up for their lack of sickness. A false cheeriness.

The room filled up. Shoulder bags dropped next to chairs, feet scuffled, people coughed and cleared their throats, some whispered so loud they could be heard three blocks away.

He wondered about the reaction if he said, "Shut the hell up!"

The quiet voice interrupted his thoughts yet again. "Do you have any trouble driving home after Chemo? My daughter's taking Finals."

Taking a deep breath before answering, he said, "Yes. It's risky. You're a lot weaker and you have the attention span of a teen age male."

That elicited a chuckle. Not much of one, but something. Enough to know he had her attention.

"Your reflexes are shot. If someone pulls out in front of you then you're going to see them sort of second hand. Like in a dream. You'll eat their tail pipe while you're thinking 'gee, I need to stop'."

"Oh dear."

"I take a taxi. Here's their number." He pulled out his wallet and searched for two cards. He copied the number from one card onto the back of his Doctor's business card and passed the card over.

"Thank you, I will call them."

That was the last of her conversation for the day. Half an hour later her poison spiked saline bags finished draining and she got up to leave. She gave a smile and nodded at him. As she left he thought; *Couple years younger than me? Late 30's maybe? Nice figure, hope the steroids don't trash that. I hope she doesn't lose that gossamer blonde hair. That would be a shame! Lovely. Guess I'm not dead yet!*

Chapter 3

The old man watched as the backhoe dug up his wife's roses. She won several awards with them through the years and tried for more. Over thirty years ago she planted the roses across the front of the yard so the neighbors could enjoy them too. Then the cancer came.

Now they were being dug up. The huge backhoe needed clearance even though his wife planted the roses out of the legal right of way.

The new neighbor's wife forced the issue. She complained to the water company about the ugly fire hydrant sticking up in her yard. "Move it" she said, "My husband is a Senator."

They told her how expensive moving the hydrant would be.

She told them, "My husband is a Senator for the State of Virginia. We deserve to have an unsullied lawn. Move it. You have yet another bill before the General Assembly to increase your rates again, don't you? Do you want his support or condemnation?"

When they notified the old man, he fought it. He even hired a lawyer to take the action to court. Eminent Domain. He sought the help of the local papers. "He's a Congressman. We are proud of our local hero."

The flowers came up and tears welled up in the old man's eyes. He had taken care of them as best he could after his wife passed on; damn cancer. But he was glad his wife didn't have to see what they did to her roses. He thought, *New neighbor's a Bitch!*

Chapter 4

The next treatment came in the blink of an eye. Although a month apart, the treatments began to seem endless. He felt a hint of his health coming back as the calendar rolled around to the next treatment date.

He sat waiting for his turn with the Phlebotomist before today's Chemo treatment and thought about the last month; *did anything good happen?*

As fast as he went downhill, he noticed the treatments brought him to a lower level each time. At work he spent more and more time with his head in his hands trying to maintain some sort of focus. *Gonna be a long summer!*

The nurse led him next to her buddy again. Not a problem, she kept pretty quiet. *Someone to lean on a bit for questions would have been nice for me too.*

"Thank you for the advice last time. I took a taxi home. My daughter drove me this time. By the way, I'm Maeve." She held out her hand.

He shook her hand saying, "Caleb; call me Cal. Glad you got home safe." He allowed a hint of a smile, more than that required too much effort.

As he sat down and rolled up his sleeve, he noticed the nurse wore the 'peaches' perfume again. She stuck him twice in his left arm then moved to his right arm and told him, "Sorry, but during Chemo, veins get harder to hit". He waited until she struck gold before he smiled.

"Is it the Chemo that makes everything taste lousy? Or am I a bad cook?" Maeve asked with a hesitant smile, trolling, wanting verbal company.

They talked a few minutes before winding down. He thought, *<u>Hard to keep an intelligent conversation going while feeling this friggin' miserable.</u>*

She showed him an article in the newspaper titled; 'Mayor's son gets probation'. She said, "Doesn't this sort of thing make you sick. Um, sicker?"

"What is it?"

"Some teenage kid swiped his parent's car. Kid drove to the local store for some junk food. He drove the wrong direction on a one-way street. Ran two cars off the road. Hit a little girl in her front yard. She got home from St. Jude's two days before."

"And they gave him probation?"

"Yeah. The kid was drunk. Judge put the blame on the booze, not the kid. Said that the kid wasn't responsible. Told the girl's parents that it was a regrettable accident. But the incident shouldn't ruin two lives."

He shook his head; half to clear it, half to show the ruling was nonsense. "Was the Judge a friend of the family?"

"The kid was the teenage son of the Mayor."

"That explains that."

"Just not right. Wouldn't it be great if the Judge got kicked out of office?"

"Yeah, it would. He's not performing his job impartially."

Conversation lapsed again.

She laughed.

Everyone stared at her. No one laughed in this room.

She caught his eye. Turning a bit pink she apologized. "I'm sorry. Great article. Poetic justice."

Not caring but trying to be polite he asked, "How so?"

"A pipe burst. A small insignificant water pipe burst."

"How's that Poetic Justice?"

"Remember the Congressman who had the fire hydrant moved?"

"Sort of. I remember some article in the paper back when I first got diagnosed. Something about an old couple and roses. I didn't pay much attention."

"Well, the small pipe happened to be IN the congressman's house. And he was on another of his fact finding missions. In the Caribbean and he took his whole family of course."

"Pretty good. A mess like that while he's vacationing on the taxpayer's dime. Nice mess to come home to. Too bad the insurance company will get stuck paying."

"That's why I laughed. They paid off the escrow account and switched insurance companies. The old company insured them through the middle of the month. The new company started coverage at the start of the following month. The water line burst after they left on the 18th of the month. No insurance. They were between companies."

He grinned and gave a little snort. "Oh that's great!

You're right, poetic justice!"

Reflecting, she said, "A burr on an old sink wrench rubbing against a nylon faucet connector. The house is ruined." The tone of her voice changed and came out harsh, "Karma's a bitch." She wore such a beautiful haunting smile he felt funny even through the haze of drugs. He thought, *Something is going on there.*

They quit talking until the electronic bell went off and the nurse unplugged Maeve from the empty bags. As she stood to leave she said, "This is Tuesday. Next Tuesday at high noon I'll be at the Panera down the street. In case you need a cup of coffee." She turned and left before he answered.

Embarrassed or feeling queasy? I think I'll try to meet her. That might make a pleasant afternoon!

Hours later he looked up the water incident up on the Internet and chuckled.

One of the papers said, "A pipe burst in the upstairs bathroom. Hot water appeared to run for the better part of two weeks. The Congressman and his wife returned home on the 31st to a ruined house."

The gentleman next door was asked if he noticed the runoff from his neighbor's house. He laughed and snorted, "Since those nasty people ruined my wife's flowers I haven't been out much. Gee, what a shame."

Cal laughed again.

The article went on to say the house was a complete loss but no one mentioned insurance.

Chapter 5

The Judge was furious and in a panic.

This was no time to be caught philandering! He was under an official review for his handling of the DUI for the Mayor's son. He needed to appear clean; at least for awhile.

He raced down the narrow street, way over the speed limit and way over what common sense dictated.

Think fast! Those were flash bulbs! Or whatever they call them these days. Are the pictures for blackmail or for the papers? I wonder if she's underage. I need to get home and call Roger. He can fix it. Oh Lordy, I hope he can fix it.

Who took the pictures? Did Roger set me up? No, he didn't know I was out. I hope she's not underage. They might remove me from the bench! Oh no, I could go to jail! Me!

He didn't see anyone in the side alley as he came barreling through and he didn't hear the suppressed rifle.

But he heard the blowout and felt the lurch of the car as he careened into several buildings. He wrenched the steering wheel and overcompensated. The car flipped, rolled, and slammed his head against the side window and then the steering wheel.

He faded in and out as EMT's loaded him into the ambulance. More flashes as more pictures got taken reminded him of his evening's tryst.

I've got to call Roger!

He heard one of the EMT's saying, "Looks like another drunk. Do the DUI Protocol."

Oh no! I can't get busted! Not me! I've got to call Roger!

He faded out again.

Chapter 6

Cal pulled into Panera early and started on his coffee and a bagel. Panera's cinnamon glazed bagels ranked high on his list of weaknesses: the list was legion.

The sun shined bright and cheery, a gentle breeze blew enough to make the new-growth leaves flutter. He no longer felt queasy from the last treatment. He sighed, *An idyllic day.*

At five minutes before noon Maeve pulled into the parking lot. *Convertible, sporty, it fits her* he thought. He watched for the flash of leg as she climbed out of the sports car. *Pantsuit, drat! I'll bet she has nice legs.* He watched her walk away from the car. *So graceful!*

As she walked in she looked around the parking lot. He saw her nod when she spotted his pickup.

How does she know what I drive?

His mind jumped gears and lost the drug induced sluggishness of the last few days. Warning bells went off. Thoughts along the lines of sex left his mind. *How did she know about the insurance? And the burr on the wrench? That wasn't in the paper. Not on the I-net. How did she know about the twosome that videoed the Judge? Is this some type of trap?* Paranoia surfaced.

He cataloged the people near him. No obvious predators, but the good ones never appeared obvious. He scanned the area; he saw people milling around or sitting and talking on phones or to each other. No one paid him any attention.

She walked in before he could leave. With a smile she said, "Hi. I'm glad you came."

Wary and on edge he stood and answered with a polite, "I'm hooked on their bagels. Tough to turn down an invite."

Why is such a pretty lady hitting on me? What is she after? What the hell is going on?

"You seem to enjoy Poetic Justice. Like with the congressman and the judge."

He decided to play it straight; a confrontation. "What are you really after? What's your game? How do you know what I drive?"

Her eyebrows went up for a second. She looked at him with a different interest, appraising. "Ahh, busted! Let me get some coffee and we'll talk."

As she went to the counter he slid his coffee to his far left side next to the booth wall. He kept his left hand curled around the steaming hot coffee, ready to launch. If she had friends coming, they would not be happy.

He thought, '*One advantage of terminal cancer; your perspective changes. If she brought friends and this is some sort of 'Game Time', things will get real messy, real fast!*'

She sat across from him with her coffee and he saw the tension mirror in her eyes. She shuddered like a visceral chill flowed down her spine; the look on her face showed apprehension!

She said, "First, I mean you no harm. Second, I wish to offer you an opportunity. No pressure, just an opportunity."

He relaxed just a bit; she mirrored him again.

"So what do you have in mind?"

"Did you read about the Judge?"

Pulling his mind back together he realized whom she meant. "You mean the one that let the Mayor's kid off the hook?"

"Yes. He got caught, big time."

"Caught with his hand in the cookie jar?"

"Not exactly his hand." She snickered and he understood. "Someone picked the lock on his motel room and someone else lit them up with a video camera. The girl was underage. The video is all over the Internet."

With a deep smile he said, "Wonderful. I love stories with a happy ending! I hope he loses his license or whatever they call it. He shouldn't be in office. I feel sorry for the girl though."

"I think she'll be okay. Her face was blacked out in the public video." She paused before adding, "Wouldn't it be great if the Mayor's kid got caught DUI in another district? Someplace the local Judge doesn't have any influence?"

"Yeah, I read that the little girl is still in the hospital. Good chance she'll end up crippled. I also read the Mayor's kid just accepted a full-ride football scholarship. He should be in jail, not running off to college."

"A group of us believe in justice. There are too many

people that mistreat others for the sake of a buck or power or whatever. They get away with abuse because of their position or their friends or because they can buy their way out."

"Like the Congressman or the Mayor's kid." He spoke with an exclamation point, not a question mark.

"Exactly."

"You were part of that." Again, knowledge, no question mark.

"Yes. I have a talent for picking locks. Almost as fast as the average person with the key."

"Why me?"

"Our group investigated you. Before retiring from the military you held a Security Clearance. Now you're a Systems Analyst at a security company. So you're reliable, you have no police record, and you are terminal."

"Are you a reporter? Or a crook? Or what?"

She gave him a small smile and answered, "None of the above. I'm an electrical engineer. I work for a private company on a government research grant. I specialize in Photo Voltaics; solar cells. But I have a part-time, ah, hobby."

After studying him for a second she added, "I don't think I've ever seen anyone so focused on me. At least not while I had my clothes on."

He never cracked a smile.

She tried again, "Okay, let me tell you some items in

confidence. If at any time you feel unwilling to keep things to yourself, tell me. I'll quit and leave."

He mulled the idea over. "Okay, continue."

"I have some friends and some acquaintances that believe people should not be above the law."

"Keep going."

"They occasionally help matters along."

"Again, like the congressman and the judge."

"Yes, are we still good?"

"Okay. Yeah, I'm good so far. You picked the lock of the Congressman's house and messed up the hose."

"I did the lock. Another person fixed the hose."

A touch of sarcasm laced his voice, "And you just happened to know about the insurance lapse?"

"His new insurance agent is terminal. The man that fixed the pipe has cancer. And you met me taking Chemo."

"Are you telling me that you belong to a club of cancer victims? A club that seeks revenge?"

"We don't seek revenge. We provide training. But you have the basic idea. Are we still good?"

A few seconds went by before, "Sure. How far are you guys willing to go?"

"Everyone's independent. To my knowledge, no one has done a drive-by shooting although we have trained several people in the use of firearms. But it's more incidental, like shooting out a street light or a car tire on a moving vehicle."

"You train people?"

"Oh yes. To us, the training is the most important part. Our *raison d'être*. We take people diagnosed with terminal cancer and help get their mind off the cancer. We train them for most anything they want to learn. Things out of the ordinary. In return, some of them – and I emphasize the word 'some' – wish to put their new talents to work."

"Who pays?"

"No one. Not in the way you're thinking. If you wanted to learn to pick a lock, I would teach you. Free. I've taught half a dozen folks. If I want to learn to shoot a rifle, I might be asked to pay for the bullets, or maybe not. Depends on who is teaching. This isn't about the money. It's about helping people through a tough time. Evening the boards give people a sense of purpose."

They sat in a companionable silence for awhile. Maeve noticed the tension leaving his frame as he thought over the implications.

Cal finished his bagel and asked, "So how does someone find out more about this?"

"Ask, but not in public. As long as you give me your promise not to compromise us, I'll tell you what I can."

He finished his coffee and said, "I have an appointment this afternoon. How about dinner tonight?"

He stared at her and raised his level of awareness: *Hint of color to her face; embarrassment? Or guilt? Touch of sweat on her brow; tense? Stiff posture; a little uneasy. Expensive very feminine clothes, blonde hair hanging loose, green eyes, smells of ...a vanilla base?*

"Cal! We-are-in-public!" Each word emphasized individually and containing a touch of exasperation.

He relaxed and asked, "What do you mean?"

"You looked like you were going to devour me!"

He nodded, "Well, that's an idea. But I'll settle for a more conventional dinner. I want to know more about you before I commit to learning about your group."

She scribbled her address on the back of her business card and said, "My house. Six O'clock." She gave him a stern look and added, "And my daughter will be there to chaperone."

Chapter 7

He arrived at her house ten minutes early. A slender teenager with fine pale red hair opened the door, the heredity apparent in the facial bone structure.

Cal held out his hand and said, "You have the look of your Mother. I'm Caleb, and most pleased to meet you." He handed her a bottle of wine.

The daughter shook his hand and said, "I'm Briana." With a smile she added, "I'll let you know later if I'm pleased to meet you." She took the proffered bottle of wine.

"Now that sounds like your Mother. I'll try to be on my best behavior."

Maeve came to the door and caught the last of the exchange. With a grin she added, "In other words, don't expect much."

He went inside and the evening went better than he hoped. The two ladies enjoyed more than a parent-child relationship. They spoke and acted as friends.

The conversations went all over; from Maeve's job, to Briana's schooling and the colleges she was applying to attend in the fall. Cal found them delightful and the meal passed too soon to suit him.

As they finished dessert, Maeve asked, "Ready to follow up on my hobby?"

Briana cocked her head to the side and said, "My cue to get lost." She gave him a steady look and added, "But not too lost."

He took that as the phrase was meant: a warning. All he could think of was, *I really like this family!*

Briana left them alone and Cal said, "You have a wonderful daughter! I'll bet she's a handful!"

"I worry about her in this day and age. So many new temptations that we never had. So many whacko's and nasty people hurting others for fun or their cause. And yes, I consider myself in the latter group. We hurt others. I have no illusions about that. The Judge that let the boy off the hook for crippling the girl; he's under judicial review. He'll likely lose his job and a big chunk of his savings. He might even end in prison because the girl was underage."

"Did you hire the girl?"

"No. Our group investigated him and followed him for a few days. When one of our people found out about the tryst, we filmed him during his next visit. Now we are trying to help the girl, a runaway sucked into the wrong crowd. We didn't set him up, we took advantage of his indiscretions. To me, that's the difference."

"How do you find out about these people? And the nasty things they do?"

"We have several web sites. Most anyone can sign in and add incidents. We have a few folks that vet the incidents. If they turn out to be substantiated, we copy them to another site. Everything on that site gets investigated with great care. We look for people who abuse their power. Although we have struck at others, we concentrate on public employees that abuse cancer victims."

"So what happens when you find someone like the Judge?"

"I copy all the information on him to a final site. This site gets viewed only by those of us who are..." she paused for the word, "active. People like me. Some incidents bother you more than others. Then someone steps up and says, 'Wouldn't it be funny if, et cetera?' Then they put forth a scenario. If enough people respond to the scenario, somebody sets something up."

"What happened with the Judge?"

"Someone said 'Wouldn't it be funny if we followed the Judge and caught him misbehaving?' Over forty of us volunteered to follow him for certain ranges of time. When we found out about the girl the instigator said, 'Wouldn't it be funny if someone picked the motel lock and I streamed them on video?' I volunteered my services. The instigator has a professional video camera that both records and streams live. I picked the lock, he took the pics, and we ran. We sent one of the original disks to the FBI and another to the State Police. Then one of our group blacked out the girl's face and hit the Internet with the video. The film went viral in about an hour. And now, justice in its own ponderous way will, we hope, be served."

Cal checked the time and asked, "I've enjoyed the day. May I see you again?"

"For me or the group?"

With no hesitation he said, "Both. I like the basic idea behind your group. I'm not sure how well my skills or, ah, level of morals would fit in with your group. But I know a District Attorney who preys on young women and makes lucrative deals with high level drug dealers."

Maeve followed him to the door saying, "Sounds interesting! Shall we start tomorrow?"

Cal smiled for the first time since the Doc gave him the long face. He felt like jumping up and clicking his heels!

He thought,
                                      The End Game's running!

Fireflies

by Elijah David

Robyn and Jade had been at it for what felt like hours, but was probably closer to ten minutes, and still not a single firefly blinked in the mason jar Momma had given them.

"I told you it's too early for fireflies," Jade said for the fifteenth time.

Robyn had lost her count somewhere after eight, but she was sure this was fifteen.

"You gotta wait till it gets warmer out."

"I'm not the one who said we should go catch fireflies tonight," Robyn retorted.

She wasn't quite sure what "retorted" meant, but she'd read it in a book a few weeks ago and ever since she'd been determined to use this new word as often as possible.

"Are too," Jade said, sticking out her tongue.

Robyn ignored her sister and turned to the open field. She remembered seeing Daddy's headlights sweep across fields last summer and all the fireflies in sight lighting up in response.

"We need a flashlight," she said.

"Do not," said Jade.

"You wanna find fireflies tonight or dontcha?"

"Yes," Jade muttered.

Robyn didn't reply as she strode off toward the house. Even in the dusky twilight, the faded whitewash stood out like a beacon. She eased the back door open, careful not to push it far enough to trigger the rusty squeal of the bottom hinge. She stretched up tall and rolled the Maglite off the shelf over the washing machine, then slipped back outside, closing the door behind her as carefully as she'd opened it.

She let her eyes adjust to the darkness of the outdoors for a few seconds, then ran off in the direction where she'd left Jade. She hadn't even made it out of earshot of the house when she heard Jade squealing with delight.

Figures, Robyn thought, *I go back to get the flashlight like a sensible person and she manages to find the only firefly for miles around without any sense.*

She clicked on the flashlight and scanned the field for Jade. A moment later Jade appeared, jumping up out of the grass like a wild jack-in-the-box.

"Robyn, Robyn, Robyn, look come see!"

"Found an early one, huh?"

Jade giggled and Robyn wondered if this was just another game.

"Well, let's see then."

Jade held up her finger and said, "You gotta turn off the light first. And don't shout. It doesn't like it when you shout."

Robyn clicked off the flashlight and sighed.

"I'm not the one who was shouting."

"Shhh," Jade hissed.

A few moments after the light went out, Robyn finally noticed what Jade had caught. Inside the mason jar a small, silvery neon glow danced madly.

Robyn leaned closer to the mason jar. The glow—it wasn't a firefly, that was for sure—was humming. No, not humming. Whispering. Like wind in the trees on a sunny day, promising thunderstorms in the night. There were words in the whispering. She felt sure she'd be able to catch them in another moment. If only she could—

"Robyn! Isn't it the best firefly ever?" Jade squealed.

"You said it didn't like shouting."

Robyn kept her voice down but made sure it had an edge to it. She hadn't said "stupid"; you weren't supposed to call people stupid, even if they were. But Jade had heard the implication.

"I just wanted to ask if you liked it," Jade said, scuffing her feet in the dirt.

Robyn ignored her and tried to catch the words the silvery glow was whispering. It was no use. Whatever she'd almost heard before, Jade had made sure she wouldn't hear it again. Maybe it was just as well. Who was to say it was something nice the whatever-it-was was whispering?

"Come to think of it, what *is* it?" Robyn asked.

"It's my firefly."

"Jade, it's *not* a firefly."

"Is too."

Robyn sighed. "Jade, fireflies are yellowish-green, not silver, and even if they were silver, you could see the bug on the other end of the light and there's no bug in the jar. Just light."

Jade stared at Robyn, then at the jar. "Maybe . . . maybe it's a what-do-you-call-it. A willy-wasp."

"A will-o'-the-wisp?"

"That's what I said," Jade replied with the tone that told Robyn she was sticking her tongue out.

"Maybe," Robyn said. "But whatever it is, we've got to let it go."

"No, it's mine!"

Jade snatched the jar up off the ground and curled around it so Robyn could only see the edges of her face shining in the wisp-glow.

"Jade, think of it like a firefly."

"But it's a willy-wasp."

"But it's *like* a firefly. And we always let the fireflies go, right?"

"Yeah." Jade's voice had that uncertain tremble that she used when Momma was trying to convince her of something she didn't want to be convinced of.

"So we have to let it go, too. If we're lucky, maybe we'll find it again tomorrow night."

Jade frowned, the lines on her forehead as deep as caverns in the pale wisp-light. "I don't wanna. I found it. It's my willy-wasp."

"Jade . . ." said Robyn, trying her best to imitate Momma's no-nonsense voice and failing.

"No," Jade said, jumping up and running off into the field.

Robyn made a noise that somehow combined a sigh, a scream, and a sob. She knew this was a bad idea, running into the fields in the dark. She stumbled over a rock set at the corner where two fields met. Then she remembered the flashlight and clicked it on, calling for Jade to stop and come back. Jade didn't call back.

Momma's gonna wear us out when we get home, Robyn thought. *Then I'm gonna wear Jade out for gettin' me in trouble too.*

Her thoughts spiraled out into smaller and smaller sentences, always focused on the same end: her and Jade home safe. She kept the image in her mind like a lucky rabbit's foot. They'd make it home safe as long as she believed they would.

It wasn't until she heard Jade scream that Robyn realized why she'd been so intent on believing they would get home safely. In the part of her heart that still believed in the bogeyman, she'd been convinced that this was a night when the bogeyman wasn't confined to the space beneath her bed.

"Help! Robyn, make them stop! Make them give it back!"

Robyn rushed toward Jade's voice, ignoring the cold as she splashed across the shallow creek at the edge of the woods.

Her heart racing so quickly she could hardly think above the noise, Robyn swung the beam of the flashlight across tree after tree. She scanned the branches and the roots, but she couldn't find Jade.

Just as Robyn began to think she should go back to the house and get an adult to help, Jade cried out again, her voice muffled and distant. Robyn spun toward the noise and the flashlight beam caught on Jade's shiny black shoe disappearing into a hole in the ground.

Somehow Robyn reached the hole without tripping and losing sight of it. She thrust her arm up to her shoulder into the hole, grasping for Jade's foot and finding nothing but air. At least there weren't any sna— *no , don't think it. If you think it, you'll never go down there.*

She didn't think about jumping. She jumped.

Alice in Wonderland is a mousing lie, she thought as she fell.

A second later she struck something solid but giving and rolled onto a lush carpet of moss. She spat the foul-tasting green stuff and looked around.

She'd fallen into a large mushroom, breaking it into five or six wedges big enough to serve as pillows. The cavern was empty except for the moss on the floor, more giant mushrooms sprouting on the walls, and Robyn. Several tunnels led away from the room.

How could she know which one Jade had gone through? And what could have taken her?

The will-o'-the-wisp's whispering crept back into Robyn's mind. What if it hadn't been the only "firefly" tonight?

Robyn stood and brushed the dirt off her knees. They were still green from the moss, but that didn't matter. She stepped carefully across the floor, as much to be quiet as to avoid slipping, and listened at each tunnel in turn. Three tunnels in, she caught sight of a familiar silvery glow. Wisps. This had to be the one.

She tore off down the tunnel, heart racing in time with her feet. She started to call for Jade but stopped, her voice croaking like a creek frog's. She didn't want the wisps to know she was coming. It would be easier to sneak Jade away if they didn't know.

Robyn followed a turn and skidded to a stop, falling back and skinning her hands and the backs of her legs on the gravelly floor. She stopped a couple of yards from the end of the tunnel. A large cavern filled with wisps opened up beyond, the combined light of the wisps' silvery bodies shining brighter than the lantern Daddy used on their camping trips. The whispering Robyn had heard earlier had grown more urgent, though it seemed hardly any louder.

If the wisps noticed her arrival, Robyn couldn't tell. The whispering never stopped. Their attention seemed focused on a spot in the center of the cavern. Robyn squinted but couldn't make out what the wisps were staring at. Then, like wind-blown rain, the wisps parted and for a moment Robyn saw Jade, her face tear-stained and her hair full of sticks and mud. She seemed further away than Robyn thought she should, as though Robyn had put on Momma's glasses. As the wisps shifted again and hid Jade from her sight, Robyn realized why.

They'd put her in a jar. A human-sized mason jar.

How was she ever going to get Jade home now?

Robyn bit her lip and got to her feet. She dusted off her legs, ignoring the sting of her skinned palms. It didn't matter how she got Jade home, she decided. Only that she got her home.

Holding out her hand to ease her way through the crowd, Robyn stepped into the cavern of wisps. The whispering changed. Though the volume never rose or fell, the feel of the unknown words shifted. She realized that the words had been angry before. Now they were curious as well as angry.

After a few steps, Robyn no longer had to shift her way through the crowd of wisps. Like Moses at the Red Sea, she walked through a clear path, the silvery walls rising above her head on either side.

Jade spotted Robyn and started crying again, her voice even more distant and hollow than before. Robyn's heart shivered at the sound, and she swore to herself she'd never put another living thing in a jar as long as she lived.

At last, she reached the jar where Jade was crouching, her arms around her knees in a stance she'd learned from Robyn last summer on their trip to Bear Lake.

"It's okay," Robyn said, her voice shaking but certain.

She didn't know how it was going to be okay, but she didn't dare entertain any thought to the contrary. "I'm here. We're going home."

"Who . . . are . . . you?"

Robyn didn't jump. The wisps had finally started speaking her language. As she'd thought, it wasn't any more reassuring than the wordless whispering.

"I'm her sister," she said, careful not to use anyone's name. She didn't remember why you weren't supposed to use names with fairy creatures, but it came up in a lot of books. "I'm taking her home."

"She . . . is . . . ours," said the wisps. "Just . . . as . . . she . . . claimed . . . one . . . of . . . us."

Robyn shook her head. Beside her, Jade whimpered that she didn't mean it and just wanted to go home. Then Jade's voice got too quiet to hear, even standing next to the jar.

"She didn't mean to do anything wrong," Robyn argued. "She would have let you go eventually. I'd almost convinced her to when you took her."

"Not . . . soon . . . enough."

The wisps shifted again, and Robyn felt her stomach twist like it did when she stared into a kaleidoscope for too long.

"You . . . may . . . leave," they said. "You . . . argued . . . for . . . our . . . freedom."

Robyn nodded and turned to Jade with a grim smile. "Come on," she said. "Let's—"

"The other one stays," the wisps said, their words so close together now they practically ran each other over. "She has violated our sovereignty. She will stay here forever as she would have kept us forever."

Robyn didn't know what sovereignty meant, but she didn't care. She knelt and scooped up a large rock, testing its weight in her hand like Daddy did when they skipped stones at the creek.

She stepped back from the jar, motioning to Jade to cover her head. "I'm taking my sister," she said to the wisps, "and you're going to have to do a lot more than stuff me in a jar to stop me."

"Do . . . not . . . test . . . our . . ."

In the space between words, Robyn slung the rock. It struck the glass and the jar shattered around Jade. Jade screamed, and Robyn rushed to her side. She pulled Jade to her feet, ignoring the broken glass, and ran toward the tunnel that had led her here.

The wisps began their angry whispering again, the volume never altering. Part of Robyn's mind, separate from the mad desire to escape, told her that the wisps ought to be musical. They were capable of it certainly, with their unified voices. Instead, they kept themselves monotone. She wondered what had set them wrong, and if there was a way to fix it.

Then they were through the wisps and into the tunnel. Part of her wondered why the wisps hadn't tried harder to stop them. They'd carried Jade off without any problem. Why did the thought of fighting two little girls instead of one change their behavior?

When they reached the cavern with the broken mushroom, Robyn realized she hadn't thought about how to get back to the surface. She glanced at the other tunnels, but none of them seemed to go the right way.

A wisp appeared over her shoulder and she swatted at it. It dodged her hand and tugged on her hair, almost dragging her off her feet. She swatted again and it flew away down another tunnel. A moment later it reappeared and flew close to Robyn and Jade, then returned to the tunnel.

"It wants us to follow," Jade said.

"That's likely," Robyn said.

"It's not angry like the others," Jade said. "It's my willy-wasp."

Robyn didn't know how Jade thought she could distinguish between the hundreds of wisps that had been in the cavern below.

"It's probably just trying to get us stuck down here forever," Robyn said. She wanted to retort something, but she couldn't think of anything when the other wisps might be coming down the tunnel for them.

She glanced back and saw that her fear had been justified. The tunnel was glowing with the distant presence of the wisps. She felt Jade's hand disappear and turned to see her sister joining the single wisp at the mouth of the other tunnel.

"Come on," Jade beckoned. "It's not like the others."

Robyn huffed and joined them. What else could she do?

The lonely wisp darted down the tunnel it had chosen and they ran hand in hand behind it. Every so often it stopped and let them catch up. When they had run for what Robyn was sure had been hours, they finally came to a place where a much friendlier glow entered the tunnel: starlight.

The wisp flitted back and forth between the opening and the girls.

"Got it," Robyn said. She pulled Jade to the hole and gave her a boost. Then she jumped and caught hold of a root poking out of the earth in the middle of the hole. When she emerged from the ground, she fell back on the dewy grass and breathed in the world. Her skinned palms stung again and she somehow felt thankful for the pain.

"Thank you," Jade said, peering down into the hole.

"I'm sorry I put you in a jar. I won't do it again. I promise."

Robyn hoped Jade remembered that promise in the morning. She took her sister's hand and led her away from the wisp tunnels. Before long they reached the dirt road that ran past their house. They were a mile or more from home, but at least they were safely above ground now.

They were almost to their driveway when Daddy's truck appeared. They waved him down and he leapt out onto the road, almost forgetting to put the truck in park.

"Where have you girls been? Do you have any idea—?"

They didn't let him finish. They were too eagerly

hugging him to hear his reproach. After a minute or two, he'd forgotten what he wanted to say.

Daddy wasn't happy Robyn had lost his Maglite, and neither he nor Momma believed her story about the wisps. But there were worse things than not being believed. Like living in a jar. Or losing your sister. And after a few days, the whole incident was forgotten.

Eventually even Jade seemed to think they'd done nothing more than catch fireflies and get lost in the woods.

Once—just once—Robyn thought she heard a whisper outside her window. Not the monotone, threatening whisper of the wisps' judgment chamber, but something cheerful, inquisitive, almost musical. She turned to the window and saw a silver flash of light zip away into the fields. When Robyn reached the window, there was no trace of the wisp. A picture had been scratched into the paint on the sill, so small Robyn had to bend almost double to get close enough to see it clearly: a firefly flying away from a glass jar.

Robyn shuddered and smiled, the memory of the giant jar giving way to the thrill of the escape and the thin, frail strength of her promise.

Gretz

by J. Smith Kirkland

Looking at my 'watch', I see numbers luminescing through the skin on my wrist, '03:05:19' . Almost time for the trial. At 03:15:00 the charge to the enclosure zone gates will be dropped. I will be led to the courtroom by guards armed with technology.

The accusations will be read by the magistrate, and the test will begin to prove my innocence. I know the outcome of the trial will make no difference. For all of the 'progressive reform' made recently, a verdict of innocent or guilty really won't change anything. The political 'Purity' movement has filled the masses with so much fear and hate that the crowds outside the courtroom will still cry for blood either way.

The guards come to the door of the room, escorting a government priest.

"Visitor for Gretz," one of them announces in a very official tone, as if there is anyone else in the room besides me. The priest walks up to the edge of my cell. He could have walked all the way over to me; the containment shield is configured so that anyone could pass through except me, but even a priest is cautious not to get too close to me. They all fear me. I have given them no reason, but the hysteria and anger needed a cause to continue, so I have been offered up as a sacrifice by the powers that be, to be thrown to their supporters to keep them ignorantly submissive.

"Do you have any sins to confess," the priest asked quietly.

"You know I am innocent of these crimes."

"We all have some sins."

"You're right. I confess to being judgmental. I am judging you for your hypocrisy right now."

He lowers his head and steps back a bit. I wish I had not said it. He has no power to save me. He doesn't even have to be here.

"I'm sorry. I shouldn't strike out at you. But you shouldn't be afraid of me either. I am different from you and those people crying for my punishment, but I am not a threat to anyone."

He looks up, and at the wall behind me, "May I pray for you?"

"If you must. But you should pray for those people outside the courthouse. They have forgotten the teachings of any god or prophet. There may be hope for them. Though there is no hope for the ones that have led them to believe their hate is righteous. Those fools are lost."

He looks down again. He just stands quietly for a moment, then turns to go. Just before he reaches the door, he stops. He turns and looks me in the eye for the first time.

"I will pray for us all."

03:15:00. A buzzer sounds. Two guards walk into the room. I do not move to leave the cell until they motion for me to do so. I do not want to startle them and have them later say I was aggressively resisting them. They walk just behind me, one on each side, all the way down the long corridor leading to the courtroom.

The courtroom is filled with reporters and politicians on the courtroom floor. There is a gallery of citizens in the back of the room. They jeer and curse me as I walk in. The judge threatens to have them removed, but does nothing more to stop their sneering remarks.

The charges are read. All lies. The plea entered. Not guilty. The test administered. It is torturous. I sit in a wooden chair. It looks like oak. It's old and worn so that the arms are smooth to the touch. The leather they use to strap my wrists to the chair arms are also smooth and worn. A virtual optical transmitter visor is paced over my eyes. I can no longer see the people in the room, and they are so quiet, I do not even hear them breath, as if they are holding their breath.

The program begins. A blinding light flashes. There is no light of course, just neural transmissions that tell my brain there is light. And then they tell my brain there is pain. Excruciating pain. I feel my muscles convulsing, my heart struggling to beat. I fight the desire to scream. Just by uttering a few forgotten words, I could release this body. I could send my essence into the judge and declare the test is over. I could let my essence float unbound into the room, and wait for the test to end. But that could mean the body dies, and I do not want this body to die yet. Death would be their proof of guilt. Five minutes. Just five minutes, but it seems like an eternity already.

The vultures in the room wait for me to scream and plea for my life. They anticipate the victory of watching my last gasp for breath, but the time has passed. My survival declares my innocence. According to their 'science', my guilt would have killed me. That is their justification for taking lives; only the guilty die, but many innocent people have perished after less than what I just endured. I am supposed to walk free now, vindicated, but I already hear the whispers,

"How could she survive?"

"Surely that is proof of her crimes."

Based on the laws he has sworn to uphold, the Judge reluctantly declares that I am to be released. He tells me I am free to leave. He knows that is the same sentence as if I had died there in front of him. The guards step back, I walk through the whispering gallery, and step outside the doors onto the steps of the courtyard. The waiting crowd gasps. Then their disappointment returns quickly to anger and hate. My thoughts go back to my first trial. The first time I was accused of crimes I did not commit. The first time I had watched the frenzy of the crowd's fury lead to my conviction over any logic or truth. I hear the same words they shouted that first time.

"Hang!"

"Burn!"

"Witch!"

I know what must be done. From the steps, I see a

raven flying across the courtyard towards me. I see the man near the bottom of the steps, with the metal cross around his neck, and the shoulder holster across his chest. He reaches for his gun. As he raises it, and the raven flies past me, I pull the hood of my jacket over my head, look down, and whisper forgotten words. I hear the shot.

The priest watches from the far end of courtyard as the body collapses into a crumbled heap on the stone steps. There was nothing he could have done. For all of the religions through the centuries that have attempted to teach love and compassion, for all the advancements in science, nothing has changed in millenniums. Hate and fear can always control the masses.

I stand beside him and whisper, "Thank you for your prayers."

He does not turn to look at me. Frozen in fear perhaps, or remorse, but not surprised. Not even startled, as if he expected me.

"Where will you go now?" sounding as if he is really concerned.

"Tonight I will be in a new city, maybe a new country, beginning a new life, with a new name."

I don't know why I feel compelled to share my plans with him. Perhaps because he has been the most compassionate person I have met since the Purity Movement came into power. Maybe it was just because I have been so lonely for so long, and someone who knows what I really am is like water in the desert.

"Maybe I will stop by Salem on my way there. My name, the first name, the one I was given by my mother, is engraved on one of the plaques in Salem, in remembrance of when I died, the first time."

Unlike so many of the innocent women and men they killed in those times, I didn't really die that day of course. I tricked them then, too. They all saw me burn in the fire, while I watched them from a distance, on the shore alone. It is almost a comfort that someone is standing with me today, watching them carry off the empty shell they think is my body. Some foolish thought inside me says he could go with me, escape what must be as much a torture for him as it was for me. But I know he has to stay. He is a warrior, and his next battlefield is waiting there on the courtyard.

"Pray for me," he said, and looks me in the eye for only the second time since we met today. He isn't even distracted by this new form I have chosen, as if he can see who I am inside.

I smile, and when he looks away I am gone. I am encouraged by the fact that there are still people like him who have not lost all humanity, out there looking for the way to end another dark age. Still, I am saddened that after all this time, people are still so foolish as to think they can kill a witch.

In for a Penny

by Calvin Beam

I was sweating in my box-like rented office like a politician testifying under oath. It was August, and despite my best attempts to get my desk fan to work by jabbing a screwdriver into the electrical parts, the blades refused to turn. In my desk drawer was a bottle of bourbon. I could trade some of it for ice from the accountant down the hall, but I wasn't that desperate. Yet.

I was still deep in that mental debate when a feminine voice waltzed across the room and cut in on my reverie.

"Hello," was what I thought I said but the word came out like the last gurgles of a coffee maker. There are women who can make a lumberjack gnaw through a redwood, and I was looking at one.

"Are you private investigator McMurtry?" she twirled.

My name is on the door and the office is big enough to hold me, a desk, a guest chair and a filing cabinet that doubles as a coat rack. I swallowed my sarcasm and nodded.

Penny was a meandering conversationalist. I didn't have anywhere to be, so I let her spill her life story. It was an idyllic childhood. Her parents sent her to Singapore when she was seven so she could work in a T-shirt factory. At 12, they moved her to Okinawa where she learned martial arts from an old Japanese guy. At 16 it was on to India, where they arranged a marriage. She was divorced at 18 because her husband didn't want to join her in the seven-year biosphere experiment her parents had signed her up for.

"Sounds swell," I said. "Any regrets?

"I never learned to carry a jug of water from the river on my head," she said.

"Everyone needs a marketable skill," I said "So why do you want to engage the services of a private investigator?"

"Oh," she said, as if the thought of hiring a detective had just occurred to her. "I want to find my twin sister, Paige. I tried using the internet to search for her but I kept getting 'Error 404, Paige not found.'"

OK, so she wasn't tech savvy.

"Does Paige have a last name?"

"Of course. Well, she used to," she said.

I looked at her like a dog staring at a can opener.

"I mean, I'm not sure what it is now. It used to be the same as mine."

I waited. She smiled and waited. I broke first.

"And your last name is … "

"Pierre," she said. I tried to wrap my mind around the perverse parents of Penny and Paige Pierre.

I looked at the remnants of my coffee and the little torn paper next to it. "Pierre like the Pierre sugar packets?"

She giggled. She actually giggled. "Like the Pierre Sugar Corporation," she said. "My parents are rich. Well, they were rich until they died. Now I'm half rich and Paige is half rich."

I'm not Stephen Hawking but I do know that half of any figure with a lot of zeroes behind it is still a figure with a lot of zeroes behind it.

"Sweet," I said, and then immediately regretted it. But my mind was already starting to envision a transmission repair for my Toyota coming out of the payment for this job. And then, dammit, my better angel made an appearance. "Don't you have a lawyer who can tell you where she is?"

Penny pouted pointedly. "That meanie won't tell me anything. He just keeps sending me checks."

I poked my better angel in the eye with the screwdriver and quoted her an exorbitant price, plus expenses. She signed a contract. And then Penny Pierre floated out of the office on a cushion of wealthy privilege.

I took a drink to celebrate, then got to work. It took eight minutes on Google to crack the case. Yeah, I timed it. I searched the society registers for Paige nee Pierre and found a wedding announcement. For a beautiful rich girl, she had married well. From there it was a hop, skip and a dark web jump to an address. It was the kind of address where the cops pull you over for driving a Toyota and then Taser you through your open window.

Screw the Toyota. I leased a Porsche and added it to my expenses.

I puttered up to the Paige Pierre Pendergast household and rang the bell. You could have knocked me over with a sugar cube when she answered the door herself.

After I explained who I was, she invited me in and browbeat me into having a bourbon with the deftly logical argument: Would you like a drink?

A few sips later, I laid out my purpose and Paige Pierre Pendergast went pale.

"You simply can't tell Penny where I am," she said. My curiosity was piqued. And then she offered to cut me a check for an amount that slapped my curiosity around like a punk and stuffed it into a trunk alongside my gagged and bound better angel.

For one month I shuttled back and forth. I told Penny that Paige kept moving and changing her name. I told Paige that Penny was closing in and I had to throw her off the trail. They kept writing checks.

OK, maybe you think I'm a bastard. Sometimes I do too. Sometimes I wonder why one rich sister wants desperately to find the other and the other rich sister desperately doesn't want to be found.

And then I sit back on the porch of my new vineyard in the south of France, open a bottle of Penny red or Paige white depending on my mood, and all those feelings just swim away.

Then I wonder if naming my vintages Pierre wasn't a bit too cheeky. But who would buy a wine called McMurtry?

It Came

by Jonathan Hixson

It watched the house from beneath the weeping willow in the side yard, perched like a vulture in the tree where the branches were best suited for climbing.

Lights flicked out as the hours dragged on until, when the moon arched its highest in the sky, the house lay dark. An hour later clouds drifted across the bone-white crescent in the sky and the yard plunged into the deepest shadow. Only then did it climbed free and prowled across the grass.

In the back, just over the air conditioning unit, the creature sank claws into the outer wall. It climbed like a lizard, the only sound the tiny crinkling squeaks of the aluminum siding under its nails. Small, agile digits scratched and worried at the window until with a shudder the unlocked glass slid up. The screen peeled away like a stubborn cobweb.

Silent and artful as a ballerina it slid in through the window and into the bedroom, avoiding toys on the floor as it settled into a crouch. The creature unfolded and crept to the bed.

It peeled back the covers and climbed inside.

Until the sky began to lighten in the east the creature

lay curled around its teddy bear, surrounded by the toys it had once owned and the memories growing harder to hold with each night.

Letter from the Front Lines

by Jonathan Hixson

Dearest Easter Basket,

The war does not go well. We have lost Halloween to the never-ending march of the foul Christmas decorations. The overrun displays of broken skeletons and bats still haunt my dreams. We fall back to Fort Easter, our sweetest and most beloved Easter, to hold the line. If we cannot stem the enemy's advance… my stitching tears at the thought! It will be left to our brothers, the leprechauns and clovers of March and Valentine's cupids, to keep hope alive.

My soul aches for you, my sweet Basket. To recline amidst your soft green grass, to cherish the many-hued eggs nestled within! One day we shall be reunited and share our secret smile at the merry pitter-patter of feet rushing towards us. Yet were I not here at the front doing battle, that dream would be forever lost to us, smothered beneath unending carols. Should I fall to the Red and Green horde, know that it was for you and for all of our good and decent kind. If this is to be my final letter, Dearest… remember me.

Your Love Strengthens Me
    Stuffed Bunny

The Quantum Mechanic

by Calvin Beam

The only reason I sat at the bar was because the tables in the back were full and I didn't have any cocaine.

At a corner table, you can see everyone who comes and goes from the Pair of Jacks bar on Seventh Street. The Pair doesn't have great ambiance, but One-Eyed Jack's depth perception issue results in a generous pour at a reasonable price and that sort of commitment should be rewarded. Diamond Jack mostly mingles with the customers, although his manner is uncomfortably handsy. He wears a diamond stud in one ear and he helps with an amateur theater company. You do the math.

I once asked One-Eyed Jack how they decided who would work on which side of the bar. "I can't watch the cash register and work the room," he said, touching his eyepatch, "and that crook would rob me blind."

So the customers are stuck with DJ, who greets you like you're trapped on a crowded subway with the world's clumsiest pickpocket.

You have to keep your head on a swivel when you sit at the bar because people who come up behind you seldom have good intentions. This is the life lesson I've taken from two terms in prison.

My name is Aaron Kalashnikov. Yes, those Kalashnikovs, makers of the world's most lethal gun, in aggregate terms. Grandson of Mikhail Timofeyevich Kalashnikov and son of Gregor Dmitri Kalashnikov. I am the middle of three brothers, so they call me AK-2. If you disregard the merchants-of-death tag, our family has quite the sense of humor.

I was on my fifth vodka — it isn't like the thrill you get from cocaine but it's mostly legal — when a hand landed on my shoulder and another felt the small of my back.

"Look Jack," I said as I turned and faced — not Jack.

"Hiya, Airy," Detective Larson Bendt said. "Glad to see you're not carrying tonight."

I felt only slightly less offended because I'd been frisked rather than groped.

"Let's find a place to talk," the detective said.

My middle finger rose. Not original, but like I said, fifth drink.

"OK, Plan B," Bendt said. He tucked a small envelope into my shirt pocket. "We can talk and you can go home with a felony weight Peruvian door prize, or I can frisk you again and you become a three-strikes offender."

"There are maybe 17 people who just saw you plant that on me."

Bendt looked around at drunks engaged in their own conversations or staring at their phones. "Maybe the bartender," he said. "But he'd make a crummy witness."

"Larson!" I said like I'd found my lost dog. "Let's talk."

Bendt cleared a private table with his badge. He ordered something expensive, which meant he wasn't going to pay. I told the waitress to keep my vodka flowing like the Volga River.

"You look terrible, Airy."

I'd already used up my best middle finger comeback, so I just drank and moped.

"I need someone with your special talent."

"You need a gun?"

"The other talent."

"You need coke?" I said, and started to pull the envelope from my pocket.

"The other, other talent."

"You need someone to solve a physics problem?"

"Exactly."

***

An hour later I was back in my one-bedroom apartment above Aaron's Garage on the edge of the city. On a clear day you can see Trenton, but there are no clear days.

I toyed with other names for my workshop. Kalashnikov's Garage wouldn't fit on the sign. And Aaron's gets listed right under AAA in the Yellow Pages.

Three generations of Kalashnikovs are engineering geniuses. I am the only theoretical physicist in the bunch, but I like to tinker.

I also like cocaine, so I pushed two piles of papers and

a half-dozen science journals to the side and dumped the contents of Bendt's envelope onto the glass topped coffee table. The only thing that came out was a note that concluded, "Magic 8-Ball says 'Ask again later.'"

Bendt is a real cut-up. There's only one piece of advice I give people: Don't ever let a cop do you a favor. It's like a payday loan with compound humiliation. Oh, and don't let anyone come up behind you. So I give out two pieces of advice.

Since the night wasn't going to end on a high, I traded sad stories with a bottle of vodka until it shed its last crystal-clear tear.

The next day I rolled out of bed about three, surprisingly without the hangover I richly deserved. Bendt's promised package was at my door, a pay-as-you-go cell phone. That checked off the first item on his to-do list. The second was to wait for a call. I don't open the garage on weekends, but I stumbled downstairs, did a little custom work on a GTO engine, and solved the Harvard physics problem of the week in my head.

Pudgy Panda delivered lo mein at exactly 8 that night and the phone rang before I had slurped my last noodle.

***

There was a table available at the Pair of Jacks, and I sat with my back to the wall. A beefy guy with a buzz-job haircut and ugly brown shoes sat at the table, also with his back to the wall. Turning toward one another created a major violation of personal space so we talked out of the sides of our mouths. It was as awkward as it sounds.

"Are you the mechanic?"

"Yes," I said, feeling like I should have had a code phrase like "the red fox catches many hens."

"What do you know about Coristan?" He had an Eastern European accent as thick as a February snowfall in Minsk.

"They make a fine carpet," I said.

"Not Couristan." He enunciated the next word clearly. "Coristan."

I struggled to try to find a difference between the two. "Next to nothing."

"Bad country," he said. "They have funny religion. They eat unclean animals. They are terrorists who want to make trouble for Berbur."

"Berber is a fine carpet," I said.

His face reddened. "Not Berber," he said. "Berbur. Are you sure you are genius?"

If I were a genius, I thought, I wouldn't be here playing tiny country Jeopardy. Instead, I replied, "What do you need?"

"There are many Cor secret agents." He hadn't given me his name, but I began to think of him as Ivan. "They think they are smart keeping identities locked up in safety box in Coristan consulate. But you, me, we are smarter. We are going to steal names."

I wasn't sure whether, as a team, we were smarter, but

I kept that to myself.

"Policeman says you have car that will drive through wall. Quarter car."

"A quantum car, yes."

He hesitated. I knew curiosity was eating him up. "How do you do it? How do you make car drive through walls?"

I rolled my eyes. "What do you know about subatomic particles?"

"Sub like sandwich or sub like boat?"

It was like trying to explain the internal combustion engine to a chipmunk. "Let's just say there is a trigger to make all the stuff that everything is made of move in a predictable way and I have that trigger."

Trigger he understood.

Now that we had a working metaphor, I continued. "If you fire a bullet at a row of tin cans, the bullet hits one or goes between them. Now picture billions of tin cans almost touching, they're always moving and you're shooting a machine gun. I can shoot between those cans. Every time."

"You must have some aim."

"I'd bet your life on it," I said.

I worked on quantum theory while I was in prison. Telling inmates it was for a car that could drive through walls kept them from stabbing me. Criminals respect that sort of creativity. And, it turns out, they're incurable gossips.

He slipped me an envelope with a hand-drawn sketch of the Coristan consulate with the vault room highlighted.

"You tell me when you're ready," he said. "Be ready by Friday. Call this number and ask for Ivan Sonobavic."

His name really was Ivan. Maybe I was a genius.

Then he walked out and stuck me with the check.

***

On Tuesday, I started to work on my list.

Some people are list-driven. Typically, I am not, but Ivan set a deadline and made it sound as if there would be a severe penalty for tardiness.

I walked to the hall of records, dug through stacks of documents, endured a slew of paper cuts and a sneezing fit caused by disturbed dust, and found what I wanted. I photographed the blueprints for the Coristan consulate. If you're going to put a car in the middle of a room in the middle of a building, it would be nice to know that your bumper won't poke through a wall.

As I left, I mentioned to the clerk that someone should make these records available electronically. She responded by turning the page of her newspaper and sighing loudly, the siren song of the civil servant.

The GTO wasn't mine, but I used it anyway to go downtown to the volunteer theater to see Diamond Jack.

DJ was a treasure trove of trivia, and among his areas of skin-deep knowledge was Coristan.

"They make great rugs," he said.

"Not Couristan, Coristan."

"Not carpets," he said. "Rugs. Carpets are what they slap on the floor of a cheap apartment."

I thought of my own beaten down brown shag.

"Rugs are what you roll up bodies in so you can get them to the trunk of your car without alerting the nosy neighbors. But don't do that with a Cor rug. Cor rugs are extremely valuable. They are made only from fibers spun from the underbelly fleece of rare sheep. They are very soft."

"I hope the sheep aren't ticklish," I said, which earned me a frown. "OK, next item."

I showed him the blueprints and gave him a page with some other necessary items. It pays to be prepared when you're dealing with the criminal element.

"A Smart car will fit fine in this room. A little snug, but you can open the doors without hitting the walls. Do you need one?"

"I have my own," I said.

He arched his eyebrows. "I would never have guessed. The rest of this stuff is pretty standard. I can have everything there by Friday afternoon."

"Don't cut it too close," I said.

He put his finger on an item at the bottom of the list "We only have two FBI jackets, though." He reached into a rack and pulled out a pair of navy blue windbreakers with big yellow FBI letters on the back to illustrate.

I volunteered to bankroll more costumes and to pay a premium for the actors' time. "I need something up my sleeve in case things turn nasty."

Diamond Jack said he could understand that.

On my way home, I stopped at a pet store. I wanted a pigeon but settled for a dove.

"There aren't any pigeon carriers in the city," the clerk said without a trace of irony. "They're just nasty."

My dove rode in a small cage in the passenger-pigeon seat. "I'll bet you're tired of being cooped up," I said. The dove didn't laugh so we made the rest of the ride in silence.

Next, I called my older brother Allen and asked him for a favor. "If you don't hear from me by 2 a.m. Saturday morning, call the state department and the cops," I said after I had given him his instructions. It was a tad dramatic, but Allen can lose track of time.

I tidied up the launch area in the garage and had just finished up when Bendt dropped by.

"I wanted to make sure you don't disappear on me, Airy," he said.

I leaned back against the gray wall of the garage and smiled at him. "Wouldn't dream of it."

I searched the Internet and found Edna Stylovich, of Cor, recently deceased. The first online translation of her obit said she was beloved by many pots full of cabbage. The second translation said she was survived by multitudes of grandchildren and great grandchildren. That sounded better.

Finally, I smoked a cigar and rubbed down my little white friend with the ashes until he was as grimy as any common street bird. If it's possible for a dove to look offended, he did.

Now it was time to set the pigeon among the cats.

***

Gleaming stone or steel buildings with large windows, high gates and luxuriant hedges line embassy row. On the next avenue over stand lesser embassies with less gleam, shorter gates and modest hedges.

Then there was my destination, a set of modest to rundown buildings with creaky fences and shrubs that hover between leafless and lifeless. This was Embassy Alley.

My walking map guided me past one dark monstrosity that looked as if it had been designed by a Cold War Soviet architect, then abandoned during construction because it was just too ugly.

According to plaque clinging to the fence, this was Berbur central. Guards eyed me suspiciously, so I gave a friendly wave to the Berburians at the gates and went to the next building, a nondescript gray affair that the hall of records told me was formerly a bankrupt bank. Between the Cor Consulate and its homely neighbor was a high chain-link fence topped by evil looking loops of razor wire. A white sign with red lightning bolts did not need translation.

"No love lost between these two," I thought.

I rang the Coristan bell and was buzzed in. An officious looking guard asked me to remove my shoes before I stepped on the rug inside the foyer.

"Is this like airport security for flying carpets?" I said. The guard smiled, then ushered me to a small, battered reception desk where a balding man was furiously stamping papers. The guard returned to his station near the door.

The room was painted a fading version of official gray. A few paintings dotted the walls and the green-and-white flag of Cor stood, appropriately, in the corner. There were several rugs interspersed over a clean but ancient tile floor.

"Coristan rugs?" I asked the official.

The balding man looked up and smiled. "No, these are from Wal-Mart," he said. "We are not a wealthy country. Rugs are for export only. My name is Rusty. How can I help you?"

He must have noticed the surprise in my eyes because he said, "Did you know that Rusty is the second-most-common personal name in Coristan, right behind Pepper."

At the mention of "Pepper," the guard by the door smiled and waved at us.

I waved back. My curiosity got the better of me. "Why are the Cors and the Berburs such bitter enemies?"

"We are not the enemies of anyone," Rusty said. "We make Canadians look curmudgeonly. However, the

Berburs nurse an ancient grudge because our prophet, how do you Americans put it, 'gangster-slapped their prophet and made him cry like a little girl.'"

"Is that true?" I said.

Rusty smiled. "Every word of it. So it is written. May I be of further service?"

I gave him my story about the passing of my distant great grandmother Edna and asked if he could retrieve more information about her so I could send proper condolences.

Rusty expressed his sympathy and trotted down the hallway, presumably to the Cor information hub.

As soon as he left, I slipped the camouflaged dove from my sleeve and dumped him on the floor. Much to my dismay, he just sat there and stared at me. I tried kicking him but the bird just did a little tuck and roll. In desperation, I bent over as if to tie my shoe, grabbed him with both hands and flung him into the air.

Finally, he flapped its wings. The noise attracted Pepper's attention. He shrieked and began to chase the bird around the room. The dove flew down a hallway and Pepper followed, still shouting.

Diamond Jack had told me that Cors found pigeons to be either demonic or delicious, I forget which, but either way it worked for me. Alone in the reception area, I whipped out my cell phone and grabbed as many pictures as I could, then started to work my way down the hall.

I didn't get very far before I ran into Rusty, who apologized for the fuss. He kindly but firmly escorted me back to the reception desk, then handed me a dossier with myriad details about the late Edna Stylovic. He offered more condolences and apologies. I was walking away from the embassy when a frightened ash-gray bird shot through an open second-floor window.

On the subway home, I e-mailed the best pictures, then deleted everything from my phone and called it a day.

***

I'll say this for Ivan, he was punctual.

By the time I turned off the 1 a.m. alarm on my phone and looked up, he filled the side door to the garage.

"Are you ready, physics man?" he grunted.

"Are you carrying cash?" I said.

He crooked his arm and a similarly bulky man pushed through the doorway and placed a canvas bag on the floor. Wads of twenties peeked through the opening. I did a quick mental volume calculation.

"Don't you want to count it?" Ivan said.

"I just did. The deal was just you and the bag, not you, the bag, and a bag man."

The bag man pulled out a gun, a winning play in most back-alley arguments.

Ivan said, "You and I come back, everybody is fine. If you come back and I don't, nobody is fine."

I nodded. "He's going to have to wait outside unless

he wants to be barbecued by gamma rays."

Both men's eyes widened. The bag man mumbled something in Berbur and left the garage. I'm not sure how far back he decided to stand, but I couldn't see him through the window.

Ivan frisked me, then ran a finger over my gray outfit. "Does this protect you from rays? What is going to protect me?"

"When you're inside the car, you're protected," I said. "This sweat suit color makes it harder to recognize me on a security camera. They've already seen me once and I don't want them to see me again"

I pulled the hood up.

"I don't care if they see me," Ivan said. "I take them all on." He patted a gun inside his jacket pocket.

"No guns," I said.

He looked at me as if I'd just called his mother a dirty Cor but he handed me the gun and I put it on the workbench.

"The steel will spark like a fork in a microwave," I said. "The car and everything inside it is a special alloy. Do you have anything else that's steel?"

He smiled. It was mostly gold. "Gift from grateful dentist."

The smile disappeared and he looked down. "I wear steel-toed boots."

I led the sock-footed Ivan to the lube bay and showed him the Smart car.

"You want me to ride in that toy?" he said. "I drive bigger golf cart."

"Fine," I said. "You just leave $15,000 for my expenses and we can go our separate ways. I'll tell Bendt it didn't work out."

Ivan decided to wedge himself into the passenger seat.

I grabbed a metal tank and a remote from the workbench. The remote went surreptitiously into my pocket and the tank went into the car's minuscule storage area. Ivan at the tank, then looked at me quizzically.

"Lock pick," I said.

I got into the car. Ivan was pale and sweating heavily.

"Buckle up," I said. "Sometimes coming out of the quantum trip can be a little rocky."

If there's a shade paler than pale, Ivan turned it. Getting his seat belt on was like trying to put a rubber band around Jell-O but eventually he managed.

"You do this before, right?" he said.

"A couple of times, although I never came out inside an unfamiliar building. This should be fun. It'll take about five minutes. Try to sit still." Then I handed him a pair of sunglasses and some earplugs.

"For extra safety, you might want to close your eyes," I said. He mumbled something in reply but I already had my earplugs in. It was show time.

With a push of the Smart car's ignition button. The car started to rise, the world went black and there was a horrific screeching, like amplified whales singing grunge band karaoke. I sneaked a sideways peek at my passenger. If he gripped the dashboard any more tightly, he would leave dents.

***

The whale song ended, a dim light returned, the car gently descended. Then there was a startling crunch of wood.

I stepped into the Coristan room of secrets and looked under the car.

"Looks like we landed on a table," I said.

"I hope it was antique," Ivan said. He gratefully discarded his seat belt and wiggled his way to freedom. "I still smell garage," he said.

"It's called sense memory," I said. "We carry particles of where we've been with us all the time. These are just more pronounced because of the fast trip and the small space."

"You call that fast?" he said.

The vault looked a lot like the rest of the consulate except for a wall covered with what appeared to be safety deposit boxes.

He studied them and pointed to number 37.

I got the tank out of the car and prepared to go to work. I looked back at Ivan and made an involuntary noise. He heard me squeal (I didn't say it was a dignified noise) and looked at me, which gave me time to grab his arm before he could put his fist through one of the paintings on the wall.

"No vandalism," I said. "Plus, I need help."

Ivan held the tank while I sprayed liquid nitrogen on box 37. When it was good and frosty, a specialty mallet and chisel cracked it like the windshield of a station wagon tailgating a gravel truck. Another smack and it was open. I grabbed a stack of papers with the Coristan seal and turned to hand them to Ivan.

I changed my mind about a direct hand-off. Instead, I dropped the papers on the passenger seat. Ivan was just zipping up after leaving a puddle for the Cors. I knew where his hand had been and that he hadn't washed.

"Let's go," I said testily, and pointed to the security camera on the front wall. Ivan turned to the camera and formed his hands into a figure suggesting a flapping bird, which I guess is the Berburian version of the middle finger. Then he folded himself back into the car.

The room went dark, the whales sang, the car rose and fell, and we were back in the garage. I breathed a sigh of relief.

***

I had done so many things right I was embarrassed about the one thing I had done wrong.

When I got out of the car, Ivan was standing next to the workbench holding the list of names I had stolen for him and his gun. I really should have locked up the gun.

You can't trust just any Sonobavic who walks into your life.

"You carry bag of money outside," he said.

"We had a deal," I said lamely.

"New deal," Ivan said.

"I can sell you out to the Cors."

Like a fine poker player, he called my bluff and raised his weapon. Grudgingly, I moved toward the bag, then flattened myself against the gray wall and pulled the strings shut on my hood. I plunged my hands into my pockets, hit the remote, and prayed.

My eyes were closed so I didn't see the expression on Ivan's face when the whales started singing, lights flashed, and I disappeared.

Maybe he thought he was disappearing into quantum space too. Maybe he was glad he relieved himself earlier because it saved his pants.

With any luck, he was paralyzed with fear.

I heard scuffling and muffled shouting in the room. After a moment, Diamond Jack shouted, "Turn that noise off."

I pushed the remote again, stepped away from the wall, and took off my hood.

Four FBI agents were cuffing Ivan. Apparently there is a clear dividing line between being willing to steal for your country and being willing to die for it. Ivan was firmly in the former camp.

"We have his buddy trussed up in the back of a car

outside," DJ said. "It's going to be a tight squeeze, but I think we can add this one. That was a neat disappearing trick. How do you do it?"

"It's all lighting and colors and refraction," I said. "Gray outfit and gray wall. I'll set one up for your theater if you ever need it."

"Impressive," DJ said.

I gave him the address of the Cor consulate and told him, "These folks will be interested in meeting your new friends."

We walked outside. The pieces of the improvised Cor vault set were stacked neatly in a pickup truck.

"We put the walls on casters to make the change quicker and smoother," DJ said, spinning one of the metal wheels with his finger. "Taking the car up on the lift was a stroke of genius. The floor just slid into place. We may not get paid, but we are theater professionals."

He beamed with pride.

"It scared the crap out of me when he went to bash that painting," I said. "The whole wall might have come down."

DJ nodded. "You are going to have to pay for cleaning the urine stain," he said.

"You didn't use real Cor rugs, did you?"

He looked at his shoes. "You said you wanted authenticity."

My cell phone rang. "You were right," Allen said. As I requested, he had stationed himself across the street from the consulate. "About 10 minutes ago, Bendt charged into the Cor Consulate like he was going to make some big arrest. Now all the lights are on and there's a lot of angry shouting in there."

"Thanks," I said. "I knew Bendt couldn't resist a double-cross. He probably figured he'd get me, the quantum car and a promotion. He'd have the payout from the Berburs for setting this up plus a payout from the Cors for catching a Berbur spy. When my friends drop Ivan and his buddy off with the evidence to show Bendt was the facilitator, they should have plenty to keep the discussions going."

Allen was quiet for a moment. "Do you really have a car that can drive through walls?" he said.

"Hell no."

A Swarm Of Flies

by Max Hernandez

"All right squad, listen up!" yelled Sergeant Stinson over the noise of the rocking armored truck. Six black battle-clad SWAT troopers stopped talking and gave him their attention.

"Fly says our next perp is one 'Julio Sanchez' of Parkdale. Single family dwelling, access door in the front, not thought to be hardened. Husband, wife, three kids." And, after a pause for effect, he added "But no dog, Sugar. Sorry."

As he had hoped, that got a few chuckles.

"He says they both purchased firearms over the past several years, so we need to be careful on this one. No reason to expect shooting, but I don't want you hurt. Clear?"

Several nods came back.

"Sugar, you take overwatch. Coco will breach. After we finish clearing, perps go to Coco in the den, everyone else on search. Here's the sheet," the sergeant finished as he sent copies of the fly to the troopers' PDAs.

Thirty seconds later, faces began to look back at him, so he yelled "Questions?"

"Blocking?" came a reply.

After glancing at his tablet, he answered "The florist van just pulled up on the street behind the house. They'll move to the edge of the back yard when we hit the curb."

"Will this be a flying raid?" came another question.

"Yes. Don't break, move fast. If necessary, Sugar will pop gas and flash through the front windows to give you cover until you reach the door. After that, lethal force if you feel threatened. Anything else?"

"Where are they now?"

Another quick check of his tablet, then he answered "Den in the back of the house, watching cable."

"All of them?"

"That's what fly says," answered Stinson. Then, when no more questions followed, he continued with: "Just a reminder: We don't get paid for damaged goods, so watch the collateral. Right?"

He got nods back.

"That means you, too, Sugar," the Sargent added with a smile. She was great in the turret, but had once gotten spooked by a barking dog and cut down an entire front porch to get at it. Gigging her about that had become a standing joke. Fortunately, she was cool enough to play along.

Eight minutes later, a black armored truck with the word POLICE painted on both sides flew down a wealthy suburban street, bounced over the curb in front of a mini-mansion, and skidded to a halt on the manicured lawn. As the rear doors opened to disgorge sprinting troopers,

Sugar swung the rotary launcher and .30-cal to cover the front windows. Fortunately, she didn't feel the need to do more, as there were no dogs around this time.

In fact, there was no resistance of any sort. Which was, after all, one of the objectives of the mission. Overwhelming force was the policy of SWAT because it saved trooper lives. Stinson regretted having to breach the door, but the damage was a small price to pay for the effect it had on a house's occupants. Otherwise, his team took his warning to heart.

Half an hour later, as he was finishing his inspection, one of the searchers approached him

"Find anything?" he asked the trooper.

"Krugerrand and a Maple Leaf," came the answer.

"That's all we need. Any trouble?"

"Nope. They were right where fly said they'd be."

"Firearms?"

"Mossberg pump in the bedroom closet, Beretta in a quick-safe by the bed."

"Loaded?"

"The Beretta."

"Good enough. Bag 'em and tag 'em," Stinson said as he made a note on his tablet before starting back towards the smashed front door. When he reached it, he stopped to check the damage. As he had hoped, the frame was untouched.

Walking onto the front lawn, he was annoyed to see two black Disposition vans just pulling up to the curb.

Didn't they understand anything about schedules?

As their crews began unloading, the sergeant in charge walked up to Stinson, who offered no greeting, but instead handed him the tablet as he said "Five perps, violation of the Economic Anti-Terrorist Act, loaded weapon present. No damage except for the front door."

"You like those doors, don't you?"

"Just sign."

"Bullet holes?"

"No shots fired. Sign."

"Don't I get a walk-through?"

"When you're on-time, you get a walk-through. Not now."

With a shake of his head, the other man signed.

Taking back his tablet, Stinson moved to hurry his troopers into their truck. The house, and the family lying on their bellies in the den, were Disposition's problem now.

Fifteen minutes later, as his black armored truck pulled off the lawn and started down the street, Sergeant Stinson yelled "All right squad, listen up..."

* * *

The room was like most the public defender used when he conducted jail interviews. Stark, scuffed, filled with metal furniture, and always painted in some variation of gray or dark-green. Across the table, his current clients, like most of the others he'd had, sat as close together as possible, even though there was room for them to spread out.

Julio and Maria Sanchez were both dressed in prison orange. Dirty, tired, and, above all, scared, they looked like two paternal twins, made alike by their circumstances. If Maria had been a man, they would have both needed a shave.

"I'm sorry," he said, though in fact an overwhelming work load had worn him into indifference. "There are few options that I can offer you. Accept this deal or go to court."

"Jail or lose everything?" asked Maria.

"Jail or parole. You've already lost everything but your children." *Which is why*, he thought, *you have me for counsel rather than someone with time to spend on your case.*

"We could fight it."

"They have you cold. You had gold in your possession, that's a felony. And a loaded firearm. Guns at a crime scene always make things worse. Fight it and you will lose. Then it's twenty years and your kids will grow up in foster care."

"Those guns were legal," said Julio.

"It's not the legality of the weapon that matters, but its presence." He got a blank stare back, so he went on. "If you broke into my office and you had a gun in your possession when you did it, a carry permit wouldn't protect you. Access is the only thing that would count because the possession of a weapon during the commission of a felony shows a willingness to commit violence. That will always go against you."

Grabbing for anything that might protect them, Maria tried "But it was an illegal search!"

"No. Sorry. A warrant was issued."

"By a secret court."

"By a legal one."

Neither of his clients said anything more, creating a painful silence that seemed to last far longer than it did. Finally, Julio broke it, almost like a good-cop bad-cop thing in reverse.

"OK. Go over the deal again."

"You plead guilty and voluntarily surrender all your assets, including all contraband. In return, you both get paroled, no jail time, and a finders fee for any contraband you surrender. You keep your kids and get a little money to start over with."

"And the 'finders fee' is?"

"Ten percent." He didn't say 'of market value' because they both understood that there was no official domestic market for gold. The valuation would be the government-set repurchase price, not the much-higher internationally-traded one.

"What about our house?" Maria asked.

"It's already been sold. All your assets have. Under civil forfeiture, they're considered to be the fruits of ill-gotten gains. This way, at least, you get something."

"Don't they have to prove anything?"

"I'm sorry," he answered, trying to look sympathetic rather than tired. "If you disagree with the ruling, the burden of proof is on you." And without money, what lawyer would ever take your case?

He let the two of them think for a minute in silence, then continued.

"As I said, they've already sold the house. But they haven't turned it over to the new owner yet. That gives you the chance to retrieve any contraband you've hidden in it and turn it in first. I advise you to take the prosecutor up on his offer, because, if you don't, and the new owner finds metal and turns it in, your parole will be revoked."

Silence returned again to the room as both the prisoners considered their alternatives.

"No," said Julio, breaking the quiet. "No conviction. Tell them we'll accept the civil forfeiture and give up our assets, but no conviction. We will not be hounded by criminal records for the rest of our lives."

"You don't have anything to negotiate with."

"Their time. I have their time. They go to court, it will cost them time. This way they get their money without any more effort. That's all they really want, anyway."

Three more cases waited for the public defender this afternoon after he finished this one. He didn't have time for this. Before he could control himself, he lashed out with "How can you be so stupid? How can you not get it?"

Then he managed to get the tone of his voice under

control, and continued with "Sorry, but you have to understand. You tried to stand up to them, tried to live your life the way you wanted rather than the way that was best for them, and they caught you at it. If they could, they would line you both up against a wall for that, but they can't, so, if they have to, they'll do the next best thing, which is to lock you up for the rest of your useful lives.

When his clients gave only silence as their answer, he hammered the point again. They had to understand, not just for their sakes, but for his because he just didn't have the time to wade through a trial.

"They have to have convictions. With them, you're just a couple of bugs. You can't get jobs, can't own firearms, can't vote, can't even oppose them in any overt way because, if you do, you can both be put back into prison anytime they want. Take the deal, it's the best you are going to get."

"Isn't there anything we can do?" asked Julio.

The question hung in the air unanswered. Their public defender struggled with his conscience. He was paid by the state, but these two wretches were his clients. To whom did he owe his loyalty? The smell of cheap disinfectant and stale sweat assaulted him as struggled with how to answer.

Finally, he said "Can you give testimony against anyone you know? Anything that would justify an investigation, would stand up in court?"

Maria looked at her husband, and he back at her. Their eyes locked in silent communication. She seemed to give a slight shake of her head, then they both looked back at their lawyer and Julio said "No."

"Think hard, because this is the only leverage you have. Can you offer evidence of any crime against anyone? Anyone at all?"

"Like who?" asked Maria.

"Acquaintances, business associates, friends. Even family. Anyone. The more powerful, the better. Because turning states evidence against something is your only chance to avoid a conviction."

* * *

Not far from where Julio Sanchez once lived, a middle-aged couple huddled in the dark of their bedroom, talking quietly about their future. Perhaps his business had collapsed, or her practice had been regulated out of existence. Or maybe one of their children had developed a medical condition that government insurance refused to cover.

The exact reason didn't matter. What did was how they would deal with the problem. Now, alone in the dark, together under heavy covers made necessary by the high cost of heat, they talked about how to raise some cash.

In spite of bank bail-ins, market failures, and brokerage bankruptcies, they still had wealth because, years ago, they had put some of their savings into anonymous assets. Even when possession of those assets had been made illegal, they had held on to them.

So now they talked about selling some gold coins.

Or maybe it was silver.

Or Bitcoin.

Never mind, the name of the asset didn't matter. What did was the fact that they conducted their discussion within earshot of one of their cell phones which sat on a bedside table.

Or maybe it was their smart TV which hung facing their bed, like a fly on the wall, that overheard them.

Or the networked baby monitor.

Or the smart door bell.

No matter which Internet device it was, the result was the same. Just as it had been in the days and weeks after this crisis started, when they used the same same kinds of words in different conversations in the kitchen in front of their smart refrigerator.

Or in the living room in front of their Google Now or Alexa digital assistant.

Or in their car within earshot of the OnStar.

Electronic microphones, like a swarm of flies, listening to every word.

It didn't matter which one had overheard them, the results were the same. An AI software robot in cyberspace identified some key words and sent copies of the entire conversations to their AT&T or Amazon or Google database system. There an NSA-installed AI program analyzed it in light of what was already recorded about them in their bank and broker accounts, phone call history, car and cell GPS location data, Facebook posts, email communications, Google searches, medical records, and NSA files. Usually, these reviews came up with nothing, but this time was different. This time the data was deemed 'actionable', and so was forwarded to a dedicated human in the local DHS Fusion center for evaluation. After looking at it, that person agreed with the computer and sent it on to legal for a warrant request and, after that, to a field unit for execution.

" All right squad, listen up!" yelled Sergeant Stinson as the armored truck lurched around a curve. "Here's your next fly sheet..."

* * *

Author's Note: Prior to the creation of central banking in the United States, the country had two forms of money: Metal (primarily gold) and banknotes (issued by local banks). The existence of the former as a monetary alternative for the general population acted as a check on the issuance of the latter because any bank which printed too many banknotes would lose the confidence of their gold depositors and suffer a bank run.

To eliminate this restraint on the newly-created Federal Reserve central bank, in 1933 the United States government made private ownership of gold illegal. Only one form of money stayed legal, that issued by the banks.

The legislation was very effective, and gold lost its monetary usage. Not until 42 years later, after the network which was necessary for gold to function as money had been destroyed by disuse and time, were Americans again allowed to own the metal.

This work assumes a new fiscal crisis has occurred in the United States, forcing the government to again eliminate any asset which might be used for money, including gold and Bitcoin, to force the public to use their debt-based offering.

Other than this one point, the physical, legal, and electronic environments described in the above story already exist.

Burnished Obsidian
First two Chapters

by Gary Sedlacek

Snowflakes and Windowshades

Irene Novacek stepped out of The Good Transmission Bar and Grill and raised her arms high to embrace the gentle show falling from the cool winter's night. She sang out to the sky: "With all of this energy, what does matter?"

She laughed and with a joyful half-turn to face Karl she said, "What does matter?"

Karl Stastny followed her out of his bar, stood next to her, and saw her framed against the two and three story storefronts of this small, Nebraska town. He smiled and said, "If you're that cheerful about all of this," he kicked a pile of yesterday's snow off the curb, "I've got a shovel you can drive tomorrow morning!"

She reached up, pushed his shoulder, and said, "I'll have plenty of that when Frank and I have chores tomorrow at home - getting chickens fed, and Frank, too, getting to our livestock in this snow." She kicked snow back at him. "Besides, this isn't so much, maybe a couple of inches and it's blowing all over the place so there's almost none out in the open."

He pulled her parka's hood over her head to shelter her from the wind and said, "Yes, well, then we'd better catch up to him and Alma and get you two home." He gestured toward two sets of footprints crossing the street in the snow

She said, "Oh, I know where he is. Don't need those tracks to take me to Alma's place." She looked across the street to the windows of Alma's second-story apartment. "They said they'd be up there waiting for us."

Karl offered his right arm to help her across the snow piled at the edge of the curb. Irene smiled and said, "Why, thank you Karl. Such royal treatment?" and she took his arm against the slick, snow-covered sidewalk outside The Good Transmission and high-stepped through the snow settled between the cars.

She said, "Deeper than it looks." She reached across with her free hand and patted his arm.

Out in the street Frank's and Alma's boot tracks meandered in front of them creating two serpentine patterns, sometimes running into each other, then bouncing off, but never too far, before coming together again.

"Looks like they've had plenty to drink," Irene said. "Think these are following tracks or were they bouncing off of each other?"

Karl laughed. "Can't tell, but the snow's pretty much filled each set." Karl pulled her arm toward him to turn her away from Alma's apartment and reached up to hold her free shoulder so she could not turn from him.

Irene tried to free her shoulder, could not, then said, "What is going on Karl? Why?"

He said, "You know, maybe we should go back to the bar and wait for them?"

"No," she shook her head. "They said to come up to her place." She tried to step away from him but he held her even more firmly.

"No, I think we should go back. It'll be warmer in the bar than at her place and we can listen to the jukebox, have a hamburger or something, and relax."

"Well," she said, "I guess, since you've got such a lock on my arm, why don't you just throw me over your shoulder and we can pretend we're living in a cave by the river?" She laughed a high, rapid laugh.

Karl released her and waved at the street, then he pointed at the clouds of light snow swirling around the lamplights. "Look at the angels," Karl said.

"Beautiful. Thank you, Karl."

He said, "With all those angels around, this is bound to be a good night."

"That would be really nice," Irene said.

She held his arm again more tightly. He crossed his hand over hers and they began again to cross the street. The light, cool wind swirled hard, fine snow around car tires and bumpers.

"The snow levels out in the street. See?"

"You know," Irene said, "I really don't think these tracks are following. I think they were made simultaneously."

"Probably. Probably Alma and Frank had more to drink than they thought and were holding themselves up and bouncing off of each other."

"Think they bounce off of each other in other ways too? Surely they can't get into too much trouble across the street." She laughed.

Karl stopped. Irene didn't stop but moved one step ahead, then, still holding his arm, swung around to face him. Karl stood still, facing Alma's apartment above the grocery store across the street. The lights were on and the curtain of one window was open and its drawn shade allowed a pale, brown light into the white street air.

Karl looked at her and, with a light laugh, said, "I wouldn't know. I try to stay out of such things. In a small town you can know too much, at least more than you want to."

"Sometimes the town's so small you can't help but know things." Irene looked earnestly at Karl.

Karl smiled at Irene, holding her hands close against the cold. He said, "You think Frank's messing around?"

"I'm just nervous. We're further behind in bills than ever and sometimes men..., you know? I just wondered if you knew anything. You and I are friends. We can talk, can't we?"

Irene saw Karl's eyes follow something high and across the street behind her. His warm grin flattened into a grim line. Karl released Irene's arm, grasped her shoulders firmly, and squared her toward him.

He said, "Let's go back to The Good Transmission to talk."

Irene hesitated and she turned her head enough to glimpse figures against Alma's shades. She broke from Karl's grip and turned to face Alma's illuminated second-story window.

Irene saw shadows of two interlaced, animated, human figures, unclothed, artistic, in the curve of eternity, grasping each other; then hands and arms slid down torsos, snaked around narrows of backs, and gently guided and pulled each torso into the other.

Irene's jaw dropped. Her eyes grew large. Her body slumped. A block of pain the size of a fist slammed into her chest. Her knees grew weak, began to give way, and Karl renewed his grip. But this time Karl slid both of his arms under hers.

She leaned back against Karl, still looking at the shadows in the window. She gasped, then paled. Panic's whirlpool swirled within her and filled her with tangled bits of memories and feelings once solid and tied together but now broken and disjointed, struggling to link again into some kind of wholeness.

Gradually, in the cool of the evening, those broken memories and disjointed feelings swirling in the whirlwind slowed and settled their shattered bits into the bottom of a place she hadn't known before, a very deep and dark place.

Everything she believed about Frank fell away, everything she knew about Frank was gone, and everything she hoped for from Frank disappeared. With their past a shambles and their present made of shadows, she knew the future they'd planned could not be.

She regained her breath; she regained her strength. Karl unclasped his hands, but held her shoulders. She knew, at least, he was still there. Then anger rose from the tornado of pain roaring through her emptiness.

She inhaled deeply, exhaled, and said, "Well...damn."

She felt Karl's hands release her shoulders and felt a soft, circular rubbing motion between her shoulder blades. She was warmed with Karl's intent even through her winter coat and she braced against the pressure of his back rub while she stared at the shadows cast against the window shade.

"Got a pistol, Karl?"

"You're kidding!"

"Nope. "

He shuddered. "Yes, I have a pistol. But you can't use it."

She turned from the window shade, looked at Karl, and met the warmth of his sympathetic eyes. She took his arm and said, "Let's go into The Good Transmission and talk."

They walked slowly toward Karl's bar. Irene slumped under the weight of her new knowledge. She felt the old world, whole and uplifting only a minute ago, dragging like a sack of potatoes behind her. Each second she held to the old world added to the sack's weight. She slowly and methodically kicked snow into the tracks Alma and Frank had made earlier that night.

Irene said, "If I can't shoot him, or her, what can I do? I have no education, no job, no income. Nothing my own."

"We all have something of our own. And a good friend will help us find it." Karl held her hand while she filled their footprints with the fresh, clean, fine snow.

Irene released Karl's arm and began freely walking beside him. She felt disjointed, lost, empty, so loose she floated, almost giddy, unweighted so much that her feet barely felt the ground.

She reached into a snowbank with both hands and brought them out cupped and full of fresh, fine snow. She scrubbed her face with the cold crystals. Her blood rose to her skin's surface and she felt a warm rush.

She rubbed a second handful around her neck and she pushed snow past her collar. It melted against her skin and formed cool rivulets that reached her depths. She found the real world cold and cleansing. She decided she would stay in it as long as she could. This clear and clean new world was better than the cozy world she'd just been forced to leave. That world had been based on lies. But the pain! How can a lie's absence cause so much pain?

Irene stopped kicking snow, and said, "If I stay here I'll have to live down the past." She looked at Karl. "But if I leave, I'll have no history and then who will I be?" She shrugged. "Before I take my first step I must see who I am."

She looked up at the swirling snow, then back at Karl, and continued, "This lie I've found tonight belongs mostly to Frank and Alma. But some of this lie belongs to you for shielding me. And some of this lie belongs to me for not seeing what must have been there had I only looked." She shook her head. "Now I must always look more closely at everything."

She walked toward The Good Transmission. "I'll probably see lots more lies in my life. I don't know what they will be or who they'll belong to."

She stopped. Karl stopped beside her. "But a lot of the lies will be mine because of willful blindness. I don't know if I can rid myself of that. I don't know if the freedom would be worth the loss."

She stepped forward and Karl steadied her as she stepped over the curb and on to the sidewalk. "But I know that to survive I must look, and my vision must be as sharp as this driven snow and as penetrating as this numbing cold."

Just outside the door of The Good Transmission she stopped again. Karl walked to the bar's doorway, turned with his hand on the door's opening handle, and waited. Irene turned to look at the windows across the street.

The curtains had been drawn. Narrow slivers of pale light escaped from the shade's edges. Irene looked away from the windows and faced the crisp air coming in on the cool breeze. She looked for the angels Karl had seen around the street lamps. The snow had stopped; the angels were gone.

She looked beyond the lamps into the clearing night sky. Against the hard, black backdrop of the winter night Irene saw stars, white and sharp. She knew her eyesight now was good enough to see clearly, when she looked. Irene understood what she'd see when next time she saw Frank.

The Good Transmission

Karl ushered Irene into a booth near the door and seated her with her back to the street. He sat opposite her and held up two fingers for Edna, tonight's barmaid, to ask for two taps.

"You want a beer," he said.

"Probably not just one but we'll see." She sighed, held her hands in her lap and looked down at them.

She said, "What did I do? How long has this been going on? Why her and not me?"

She lifted her arms, placed her elbows on the edge of the table, and, still looking down, cupped her forehead in her hands.

She said, "So many questions I don't want to ask. I don't know if I want the answers."

Edna spotted two coasters in front of them. Karl moved Irene's with her beer against the wall.

He said, "Nobody wants to ask those questions. Much less answer them."

He sipped from his glass. "Maybe the people who violate that trust have answers, or maybe they just have excuses. I've never seen this happen where the harm it causes is justified."

He took a napkin from the holder along the wall and placed it on the table in front of Irene. "A little honesty goes a long way to stop a lot of pain. Why don't people know that?"

Irene said, "They know it when the hurt is done to them but they ignore or deny it when they're doing the damage."

He said, "Seems like."

She took the napkin he'd placed in front of her and wiped her eyes.

He said, "Is there anything I can do to help?"

Two customers walked by, nudged each other, and one muttered, "Missed it by a day."

Irene looked up. "What did he miss by a day?"

Karl said, "I wouldn't worry about that if I were you. You had nothing to do with it."

"Come on Karl. Is there something else that I've missed?"

"In the interest of that honesty we were talking about?" He took another sip of his beer. "Some of the guys had a pool. They drew numbers and the winner picked the number of the days it took you to find out about this."

She dropped her head back into her hands and rolled it back and forth, then slapped her hand against the wall next to her.

"Isn't there any respect in this town?"

"Well," Karl said. "It is a small town and it was just a few guys."

She glared at Karl. "So what did you have to do with this?"

He waved his hands in front of him. "Nothing.

Nothing. They wanted to put the numbers in my safe but I said, 'No.' Told them personal tragedy is not a game and I'd have no part of it." He took a napkin for himself and wiped his mouth. "They just went to another bar."

"So you only lost some business, is that it?"

"Probably, but I wasn't going to put up with that."

"You knew this was happening and you didn't tell me."

"That's right." He looked at her evenly. "I knew about the pool and I knew Frank and Alma were screwing around." He took another sip of his beer. "I had three choices. I could tell you and maybe be wrong, or I could let it go and maybe it would stop before you found out about it, or I could let it go and wait until you found out and let you take the lead." He paused and glanced at her.

She said, "And?"

"If I told you and I was wrong or couldn't prove it there would have been a big stir about nothing and you wouldn't have trusted me. They would have lied about it. They might still do that, or try. And then you probably would have believed them and not trusted me." He shrugged. "But now that you know, the issue of the reality is decided."

She shook her head.

Karl continued, "So I lost any way you look at it." He folded his napkin and wiped the table in front of him. "This is a losing situation for all of us."

Irene said, "Why am I sitting here? Why should I trust you? Now?"

"I don't know. You have to decide that. I can see how much pain this has caused you. I share some of that pain. I understand it, where it comes from."

She said, "Karl, that first time you showed me what the stars looked like through that telescope you have on the roof I saw a world that has not closed with this." She wiped her eyes and held her head in her hands and her shoulders began to shake.

They sat silently for a minute. People walked by and hesitated and gestured toward Irene, extending their hand as if to comfort her and looking at Karl for approval. He waved his hand in dismissal and smiled in thanks and they walked on.

"Irene," he said, "this kind of thing, in a small town. If you keep it to yourself the problem is yours and so is the pain and struggle. But when everybody knows what is going on, once they know you know the truth, they can be open with you and they will be there to help the pain disappear."

She said, "So that's supposed to make me feel better?"

"No," he said. "Less self-conscious maybe, and more optimistic. But it won't take away anything about your feelings about Frank or Alma."

"And you?"

"I know you're pissed at me," Karl said. "And I'm truly sorry you're disappointed in me for not telling you, but what good would it have done? What would you have done?"

"Same thing as now - nothing, at least not right away.

I need time to think. And the more I know about what this is the more clearly I can think about it, so it is a blessing, I suppose, that you have known - because now you can help me fill in the blanks, if I can trust you."

"Well, you know I didn't participate in the pool so that should tell you something."

"Ok, let's get past that. Tell me what you know."

Karl glanced at her and then looked away at the row of barstools tucked beneath the bar's brass rail.

She said, "Don't spare me, please," she said. "I don't need any sparing tonight. Things are already raw so this is the time for all the details, please."

"Alright." Karl cleared his throat and took another sip of beer. "This has been going on for several months. One day he came in here and got drunk and complained bitterly about having to cut his corn for silage."

She said, "He hated cutting that corn early, but the four years of drought we've had dried us out so badly he had to do something to save some part of it." She took another sip of her beer and placed it on her coaster with a thunk. "That was a lot more than 'several' months ago. That was in early August so it's been going on for more than seven months!"

Irene pointed at Karl.

"Don't spare me!"

She closed her fist and dropped it to the table. "But we were lucky to have anything to cut then. It's more than a lot of farmers had."

Karl said, "You sound like that was a good thing but

he made it sound so bad."

"Silage can't be sold like corn so there it sat, in those pits, and we had no cattle to feed and then I found out we didn't have money to buy cattle."

"So that's why he was so far down about it. No one knew he was so short of cash and credit."

"He kept that secret close." She shrugged. "He didn't even tell me."

"So he - you both, on the farm - have been in a slide since then?"

"Yes."

"Well, that silage in August was what put him over the top where Alma was concerned. That was when it all started."

Irene said, "He hired her to help me with the meals for the harvest crew. You know, I thought she took longer than she should have taking lunch to the field. When I asked her about it she just said she had to wait for some of the guys to finish their rounds."

Irene compressed her lips into a thin, tight line. "And since then she's acted like a friend."

Karl said, "Irene, I know that she valued her time with you."

"For what? So she could set me up? Pump me for information? Make me feel like I meant a lot to her while she was screwing Frank? What kind of help is that?"

"I don't know," he held up his hands. "I don't know. She always brightened when she talked about your time together."

"Can I trust that now?" Irene shrugged. "And the other stuff," she looked askance at Karl. "I don't know how much you know about the other stuff."

"Once she and I did a good luck ceremony." He slid his beer on his coaster a little to his left. "Seemed to me some kind of witch craft, sort of spooky. Nothing devilish, but it was different."

"Yes." She shrugged. "Wicca. At least that's what she told me. A sort of white magic that works toward wishing people well. Not the kind of magic that wishes harm on people. She said it's based in the natural world, all about our being with the earth and sky, Mother Earth and Father Sky." Irene sipped her beer.

Karl said, "Think that had anything to do with her taking on Frank? She's had all kinds of offers from a lot of men around here but she's stayed away from them."

"Did any of them go for her mystical stuff?"

"No, come to think of it. When she talked about those stones of hers they all backed off."

Irene raised her eyebrows and said, "You know, once she told me she could tell what people were feeling just by having them hold a stone. Said she had some in a box behind the bar she used sometimes - that a black stone worked for Frank."

"That's probably it. He was the first and only guy in the area who would listen to her mysticals." He paused and looked at her. "So, what are you going to do? Take a baseball bat after them?"

Irene shrugged.

"I should, I suppose, do something like that. But you know, how would that change anything? Seems to me it'd just make things worse."

She slumped further in her seat and looked at Karl.

She said, "So much of our world has collapsed during this drought. Friends selling out and moving to towns to work in manufacturing plants. We'll likely join them, so our dream of a farm is gone. All those decisions Frank made and then this drought makes any gambling, what we once called investing, just stand out as a failure. We're failures."

Her shoulders began to shake again, just a little.

"All the future we had planned," she waved her hand in front of her, "just gone."

She pulled another napkin from the dispenser on the table and wiped her nose, then lifted another to her eyes.

"At least we had each other. Until tonight." She reached for another napkin and said, "Eight years of marriage and hard work - just gone."

Karl said, "I wish I could do something to help."

Irene dropped both hands to the table in front of her. "What could you do - you're a man. Aren't you just like him? Wouldn't you do the same?"

"Irene, Frank's life was broken and he felt he had to protect you for as long as he could. Doesn't that count for something?"

Her upper lip curled and her voice became more intense.

"He picked one hell of a way of protecting me."

"I'm not saying he did the right thing. Just that he had a lot of pressure too."

"Like I said, wouldn't you do the same?"

Karl shrugged. "Who knows what I'd do? There are farmers with less pressure who have committed suicide. Would that be better?"

Irene took a long, slow sip of her beer.

She sighed, "I suppose you're right. Only so much a person can do." She looked down again and tears crawled down her cheeks. Without lifting her head she looked at Karl. "But why did he have to screw her? Why couldn't he tell me about our problems? He and I might have gotten something done!" She lifted her head and squared her face with his.

He said, "Lots of men can't do that because they're taught they wouldn't be men if they couldn't handle things on their own. Frank's dad, I hear, was more this way than Frank is."

"So, look at his dad? That's how I was supposed to know I married a man as sensitive as an anvil?"

"Yes."

"Well, next time I'll know that."

"Next time? So you've decided what you're going to do?"

"No, not for sure." She looked down at the table again and traced the outline of the coaster with her index finger, then said, "But I can't count on him to help me here. I have to go through this on my own."

Her eyes followed the length of the long bar on the far side of the room, then jumped to the mirror behind the bar and the lighted beer advertisements hanging on the wall above the mirror. "Never thought this would happen to me. Never prepared for it." She looked across the back of the bar to the pool tables and shuffleboard game, then said, "So I must at least learn from it."

She looked back at Karl. "I will not use your pistol on him; nor will I use a baseball bat on them. But I will try to learn as much as I can. I need to know from them."

She took another sip of her beer. "I can deal with Frank, probably will tonight. But Alma? I want to know what she's really like. I can't imagine doing this to another woman. But this is still new territory for me and who do I trust?"

"Trust me? I want to help."

She withdrew, became smaller in her side of the booth.

He said, "Remember, that night on the roof when you looked through the telescope at the moon?"

She nodded.

"Like you said before, I introduced you to a new world then, and you were amazed by it - your first look through a telescope and your first look at the moon and its craters, and all that light and energy out there in the universe." He stopped talking.

"And," she said.

"And you said we seemed, even then, even when I'd

been in town less than a year, that we seemed to know what the other was thinking."

"Yes, I remember saying that."

"Has that changed?"

He waited for a response. There was none.

"Well, it has not changed for me. I want only the best for you. If that means staying with Frank, then so be it. If that means leaving him, then so be it. I want to help you through whatever you decide. No strings."

Irene relaxed, looked up at him, and said, "You know that right now you are the only thing keeping me from flying off this planet."

They smiled at each other.

Irene said, "You are helping me, if only just by staying in one place and listening." She reached for another napkin and cleared her eyes. "I'd guess you get a lot of this over the bar?"

He extended his right hand toward her, palm up, on the table, "Not ever any I wanted so much to be able to do something about."

She reached out her hand and covered his, patted his open palm twice and withdrew hers.

"Thank you, Karl. Thank you."

He withdrew his hand. The Good Transmission's quiet conversations and low-pitched chunking of beer bottles settling on the bar and tables dulled to nothing as they sat, locked eyes exploring each other, in silence that thickened and grew and wrapped around them. They closed their eyes and sat with each other in the low glow of a meditative sympathy, a bridge of light that extended across the table with enough strength to surround them and warm them without heat; they communicated without speaking, knew without thinking, existed without touching. They became energy without form and created from their disparate selves one pool of life.

Martyred Justice

Introduction

by Blaire Adams

  Buttoning only the top in a row of five, as she smoothed the wrinkled sleeves of last year's all-weather jacket, Lulu Waterton stopped short. The air hung heavy with the weight of a foul odor dredged up by the pumping of silt from a nearby pond – its stench temporarily camouflaged by the brief rain shower an hour or so before. Stepping over a shallow puddle covered with iridescent bands of green and blue, she was glad she'd taken the time to put on her galoshes, even if they did pinch her calves. She tried not to be distracted.

  Furls of the frayed crimson scarf dangled around her neck in opposition to her otherwise nondescript attire. The compensation of a warm neck had been little compared to the pain her arthritic fingers endured as she tied a knot in the wide band of red. By general appearance, she was not a woman to be remembered. Knowing this, however, had never bothered her; in fact, she'd been comforted by it. Most of the time, she kept herself to herself; but, sometimes, there were instances, where she had no other choice but to interact with those around her. And, whether she wanted to, or not, this was one of them.

In quiet judgment, she found most people in this "Mayberry" community to be nothing more than fools with newfound money. On Sundays, she watched as they dutifully aligned their vehicles aside one another in the church parking lot across the street from her house. The commonalities of their occupants were undeniable. With quick steps and selected finery, they rushed in their pursuit of an undesignated church pew upon which they sat for the full hour it took to reset their moral compasses.

Then, at 12:15, she watched again as those refreshed by the hopeful and forgiving words of the pulpit, meandered toward their cars with no apparent purpose other than to go home and enjoy a Sunday dinner. While mothers mandated their older children to meet them at the car, fathers took off their jackets, lit up cigarettes and took one long last puff before discreetly grinding the ash into the mottled pavement. The intensity on their faces had softened and would stay that way for the next hour or so, until they were reminded of the required pace to maintain their pretense as "pillars of the community." It was almost comedic.

By contrast, what Lulu Waterton was witness to now was no comedy. Looking at the shape of characters whose strayed lives stood before her, she found herself uttering the family mantra for self-control. *When folks back home tell this story, what difference will it make?* Chanting it softly seemed to strengthen her position.

Lulu was a woman of fierce determination. Her grandmother, Ora Latham, had been the family storyteller. Every family has one; but somehow, in spite of her legendary accounts of family mishaps, Ora had managed to uphold her pledge of secrecy to those who valued it most.

As a woman alone, it was from these same stories that Lulu had harnessed her will and strength to win the challenge of life in areas where others would likely fail. Things were so different back then.

She ran her fingers through the sparse strings of her thinning hair and gathered herself to answer the questions that were, no doubt, inevitable.

"Miss Waterton, could you step over here for a minute?" She was shaken by the sound of a voice outside her head. "We'd like to hear your version of what happened here."

Offering a weak smile that conveyed both cooperation and vulnerability, she walked steadily over to the officer. Beside him stood two other men who were not in uniform. The impatience in their postures told her they wanted to leave, but the curiosity in their faces had won the argument and urged them to stay a little longer.

The uniformed officer was at least a foot taller than the others, a physical asset which automatically translated into an air of authority. Lulu knew the physicality of her five-foot-four inch stocky frame was no match in the contest of acceptance among the many gawkers.

When folks back home tell this story, what difference will it make?

The loop played slower in her head now, as if trying to give her time to think. She thought about the fathers who drove their families home from the Sunday church services, and instead of a sense of comedy, it gave her a feeling of calm. If their pretense could be "pillars of the community," why couldn't hers? Above all, she had to remember how the details of tonight's happenings might be detailed in the future.

"Miss Waterton! Miss Waterton! Are you all right? Do you feel like answering a few questions for us?"

It was as if the tone of the officer's voice had been the additional one that her mind just couldn't accept. Her steadiness was beginning to unravel and she found herself listing to one side as if there was some kind of wall supporting her but suddenly began to give way.

The blackness had enveloped her again, and as its dark warmth surrounded her, she was comforted by the image she saw of herself as a younger woman. There was no heaviness in her step or soul. The lines in her face had disappeared and her body was made of angles rather than the roundness it had grown into. Instead of the sensible bob style in which she now wore her hair, long dark locks swayed with her every movement.

As the weight lifted from her soul, she noted the slight movement of something just beyond her reach. There was a child. She could see its light blonde hair. It appeared almost white in the hazy glow that surrounded it.

"Miss Waterton! Wake up Miss Waterton! Are you all right?"

The sound of voices surrounded her – some of them understandable, but most not. The comfort of the blackness around her was interrupted by the feeling of pressure on her arm.

She stirred, but was unwilling to leave the repose of her current state. It was safe here. Her body was younger and her soul more spirited.

The reassuring touch of a hand gently made its way into her own. What was that smell? Floral. Some kind of flowers around her.

"Have I died? This must be what it's like," she thought. "They got it backwards. You're healed *first*, and then you die" – just as she'd been taught in the fundamentalist church, God accepts nothing less than perfection.

Again, the flowers. Her eyes opened with reluctance as she felt her body being straightened against what felt like some kind of cold, hard steel. Was it a gurney? No, she wasn't lying down.

"It's all right, Miss Waterton. You're in a safe place. You can wake up now."

As if to prepare herself. she drew her breath in slowly. The tow-headed child stepped out of the moon's glow; and, instead of a plea for its return, a guttural moan escaped from her throat.

Where had it gone?

About The Authors

Blaire Adams

As a professional ghostwriter for over two decades, Blaire Adams, has long been a master secret-keeper. Through her previous airline employment, good fortune came to her one evening when she had the privilege of escorting an acting legend to her connecting flight. With the initials of "LB," this actress decided to turn the tables on Blaire by chatting *her* up – instead of the usual other way around. After perusing excerpts from her personal writing and promising to "put it in the hands of the right people," Blaire acquired a literary agent within the next week. "LB" had kept her promise. To date, Blaire has over 25 celebrity memoirs in her ghostwriting repertoire.

Blaire has played an active part in the campaign for women's rights for almost 30 years, and is well known among the principals of that movement. In 1996, she was a guest on the Oprah Winfrey Show as it examined the issue of an "appropriate amount of working hours" for both custodial and non-custodial mothers. Later in 1999, in addition to being recognized by then-President Bill Clinton, she was appointed an Honorary Kentucky Colonel for her work on both state and federal levels in the protection of victims of domestic violence.

Professional writing affiliations include holding offices as Regional Director, Treasurer, and Conference Coordinator in New Jersey, New York, and Florida, along with facilitating writers' groups in almost every state she's resided. Her trademarked writers' groups include Creative Scribes© and Musing Wordsmiths©.

Having published articles in several Chattanooga magazines, including "Women's Way Journal," "For Women Only," "Homes & Living," she was a featured author in "The Times Free Press," in 2008, and wrote a monthly syndicated column on Domestic Violence Prevention Awareness Education for a subsidiary of the Times-Journal, Inc. newspaper organization for three years.

More recently, she and her faithful Scottie, Quincy, have taken up residence at their newest writer's cottage on Signal Mountain, TN where she can pursue the completion of a more personal project, "Martyred Justice."

facebook.com/blaire.adams.359

twitter.com/Blaireadams1

blaireadams.blogspot.com

blaireadams.com

Calvin Beam

Calvin Beam was born in Philadelphia and received his bachelor of journalism degree from the University of Missouri. He survived a 30-plus year newspaper career with his sense of humor intact, although the same cannot be said for his retirement account. He lives in Chattanooga, Tenn., where the pace of Southern life suits him just fine.

Elijah David

Elijah David lives, works, and writes in the Chattanooga area. He is the author of *Albion Academy*, the first book in the Albion Quartet, and his stories and poems have appeared in publications from The Crossover Alliance, Oloris Publishing, and Troy University's *Rubicon*.Though his only magical talent is putting pen to paper, Elijah believes magic lurks around every corner, if you only know how to look for it. He and his wife are busy raising a small Hobbit and a calico cat. Elijah David can be found online at

elijahdavidauthor.blogspot.com
facebook/elijahdavidauthor
goodreads.com/author/show/14746895.Elijah_David
pintrest.com/elijahdavidauth

Gary Sedlacek

Gary Sedlacek and his wife live near Chattanooga, TN. He has submitted here the first two chapters of BURNISHED OBSIDIAN, a novel about people in the Midwest resolving themselves against a background of economic and social change.

J. Smith Kirkland

J. Smith Kirkland grew up in a haunted house in Dallas Bay, TN. This probably contributes to the fact that his fictional stories revolve around fate, ghosts, witches, and legends. His "Tales of the Catalin" series can be found on Amazon along with his essays in collections like "Growing Up Without WiFi"

Johnathon Hixson

Jonathan Hixson makes words. He's published nearly a dozen stories, most of which are in the Furry Fandom, as well as edited close to ten anthologies at this point in time. When not trying to dredge a few words out of the molasses-like motivation, he is yelling on the internet. Oh the internet.

Kelle Z. Riley

Kelle Z. Riley, writer, speaker, global traveler, Ph.D. chemist and safety/martial arts expert has been featured in public forums that range from local Newspapers to National television. In addition to her works of fiction, a personal story was included in "Chicken Soup for the Soul: Living with Alzheimer's and Other Dementias." Her other publications include a romantic suspense (Dangerous Affairs), multiple short stories, a self-published memoir in honor of her father, and the newly released Undercover Cat Series books: The Cupcake Caper and Shaken, Not Purred which feature a scientist-turned-sleuth. The Tiger's Tale, the third book in the series will be released in January 2019. A former Golden Heart Finalist, Kelle resides in Chattanooga, TN. She is the past program chair and popular speaker for the Chattanooga Writer's Guild, a member of Sisters in Crime, Romance Writers' of America and various local chapters. When not writing, she can be found pursuing passions such as being a self-defense instructor, a Master Gardener Intern and a full time chemist with numerous professional publications and U. S. patents. Kelle can be reached at

facebook.com/kellyzriley

twitter.com/kellezriley

kellezriley.net

Max Hernandez

Max Hernandez specializes in technically-accurate fast-paced fiction which explores how debt money, the Internet, and the surveillance state have collectivized the economic and political relationships of our lives as well as illustrate what we can do to fight back against that enslavement. His first novel, **Thieves Emporium**, received an average rating of 4.6 from over 130 reviews on Amazon. It was also serialized by **The Daily Bell** where you can start reading it for free beginning at thedailybell.com

Peter Sculley

Pete Sculley and his wife built their dream home to be amid the woods of Lookout Mountain in Rising Fawn, Georgia. After taking early retirement, Pete has been able to focus on his life long passion for reading and writing. He shares his stories to entertain us and for his own enjoyment.

Made in the USA
Columbia, SC
08 February 2022